# JEN FINELLI, MD

# Heartbeat in the Hallways

## *A Scifi Fairytale*

*Who says time is money*
*My time is more valuable than that*
*Agust D*

# Contents

# Don't forget to claim your audiobook-mini!

This novella comes with a FREE full-length audiobook-mini, read in its entirety by the author.

That's like going to a special signing for free, or maybe getting a fiver slipped into your pocket by a stranger—audio, whether music or story, usually goes for several bucks an hour at minimum.

But you get yours just for picking up this book.

> *Head to http://byjenfinelli.com/heartbeat-in-the-hallways and click I OWN THIS BOOK to get your free audiobook accompaniment! ^_^*

Just as a little thank you surprise. You see, the purchase you made here helps me save up for a number of important charities, like Isabel's orphanage and a Paraguayan clinic for the needy. So I figured I'd just thank you a little extra for what you've done!

> *Once more, that's http://byjenfinelli.com/heartbeat-in-the-hallways and click I OWN THIS BOOK. See you there!*

~Jen Finelli, MD
byjenfinelli.com

*Jen Finelli is a world-traveling scifi author who's ridden a motorcycle in a monsoon, swum with sharks, crawled under barbed wire in the mud, and hiked everywhere from hidden coral deserts and island mountains to steaming underground urban tunnels littered with poetry. She was once locked inside a German nunnery, and recently had to find her way through swamp-filled Korean foothills dotted with graveyards on Friday the 13th under a full moon without a flashlight. No joke. On her quest to rescue stories often swallowed by the shadows, Jen's delivered babies, cradled the dying, and interviewed everyone from prostitutes to Senators.*

*You're welcome to download some of her stories for free at byjenfinelli.com/you-want-heroes-and-fairies, or join her quest to build a clinic for the needy at patreon.com/becominghero. Jen's a licensed MD, FAWM candidate, and sexual assault medical forensic examiner—but when she grows up, she wants to be a superhero.*

# Upper Synovi

Rayn was an unremarkable jerk in a remarkable world—until his kidnapping.

Every night while he slept, the living hallways outside his room grew, creeping through his floating city to form the streets for tomorrow.

Every morning, the hallways clicked, Rayn's alarm beeped the chip-tune national anthem, and he tumbled out of bed, scurried like a hamster through his shower-tube, and stepped out his door into a new spongy corridor dressed in the silver robe of an up-and-coming young professional.

He never rose early enough for breakfast and never gave himself time to think.

*I'm a cell in the body of an organismal city* never occurred to him, for better or for worse.

This morning—the morning of his kidnapping—as all mornings, the hallways pulsed red. Translucent crimson spherules with black irises blinked here and there in the walls, cameras watching the flow of human life. The floor quivered, packed down under thousands of bare feet, and where the majority of the feet turned, the hallways grew to carry them. The ceiling above Rayn rumbled with the footsteps of thousands of adults, and on the level below scampered thousands of children, unseen and forgotten by their young adult elders except for the brief moments when Rayn could hear them fighting.

The chip-tune music stopped playing.

Rayn's heart jumped; he sucked in his breath and dove into the nearest square hole in the wall. A hatch latched shut behind him *just* as he slid through—his hands and knees skidded on smooth tiling as he tumbled down a short chute into a vast white classroom with a one-eighty view out into the monotony of space.

*That was close.* Rayn scowled as he stood and stretched his back. No one wanted to be stuck out in the hallways alone.

Rayn shivered as he looked around for an empty seat—drat. Out of two hundred egg-pods scattered among the potted plants only one remained empty, which left him to sit next to Voni, the weird platinum-blond guy with dark skin. *I really need to get here earlier.*

"Hey again," said Voni, waving through the window of his pod.

"Hey." Rayn slid into his own pod and laid his palm on the front wall to activate it. He pretended not to hear Voni after that. Voni was soft like the city streets, and squicky in the head, and while Rayn felt bad for the guy, he didn't want to talk to him alone. People might think things.

The walls of Rayn's egg-pod slurped as they connected with the nerves in his hand; information bled around him as he laid back his head and felt the cool surface meld and flow through his hair to synapse with his mind. He closed his eyes as concepts, pictures, graphs appeared…

"Dammit, statistics again?" Rayn muttered. "Why does the law program even have maths?"

Voni's voice floated to him from outside the academic dream, responding to Rayn's complaint with something distant about well-rounded curricula. Something preachy. Computer-science-y. Rayn didn't bother portioning off any part of his brain to answer.

Something flickered.

Another coding error? Rayn grumbled under his breath as he delved deeper, beyond the math assignments, into the main control panel of the egg. His hands tingled; he fingered through the pod's connections and programs, searching—definitely no virus here.

But everything flickered again. An eerie redness spilled over the statistics graphs. Rayn's heartbeat rose—and then the color vanished.

Rayn studied in peace for a few minutes.

Then, again! Static, a scattered image—Rayn's vision jumped to the dark hallway outside. Crimson shadows overlaid the soft glow of the pulsing walls. Empty.

Wait. Rayn cocked his head, straining to hear. A fast, light heartbeat, down the hall. The soft, still squish of a tiny footstep left no print on the pliable floor. No body...

Wait! There! A thin, translucent face floated in the distance, coming around the corner. Dark eyes turned towards Rayn; for an instant, gentle lips sang out a haunting call.

Rayn jerked back, ripping his hand out of connection with the pod. Pain tingled up his arm as he cursed and shoved it back in. Someone's stupid ghost-movie was interfering with his personalized learning program. That someone, or maybe the computer programmer who'd allowed the interference, needed a word from the Plexus.

With a twitch of his finger Rayn reported the bug just as the chip-music began again. Rayn jolted upright like a boy awakening from a nightmare; a flash of heat ran down his fingertips and spine as the pod released him and he climbed out. The hatches to the hallways popped open.

"Did you get anything done?" Voni asked as the herd began to migrate again.

"No. Been stuck on the same program for the past two days. Bug. Your fellow computer nerds can't get their act together," Rayn growled. "Hey, you wouldn't happen to know where we're going next, would you?"

"I think we have a group project?"

"Finally." Rayn sighed in relief. Two heads worked better than one and Rayn believed, without a breath of doubt, that solitude of any kind killed neurons. The herd kept each other sane, filtered ideas, and cooperated to form a greater whole. People became weird alone.

Like Voni.

The music stopped. Everyone ducked into another series of square hatches, some to learn visual arts, some chemistry, culinary skills…cooking had been Rayn's favorite back in the day.

A waste of time. Now, he just wanted to graduate to the adult level and start his career, and a mountain of science classes stood in his way.

*This* room held thirty onyx tables scattered at random intervals, each decorated with one velvety-pink potted plant. An older man descended from the adult levels on a hydraulic tube.

"We have a professor today!" Voni's smile grated on Rayn's already itching nerves. "I think I'll go talk to him and see what's going on upstairs."

"No, please don't," Rayn begged. "It looks so juvenile when you suck up to the prof before he's even started. He hasn't even done his job yet—there's no way for you to know whether or not he's any good!"

"He doesn't have to prove himself before I *talk* to him."

"No, see, that's where you're wrong. He does have to prove himself. You use your time with people who are worth it. It's an economic exchange—that's why it's called *spending* time. You need full value for what you spend."

"And you're getting your full value over there with Wyn?" Voni laughed. "That's where you're headed, right? To use all that valuable breath to leer at the ladies? What does your girlfriend think about that?"

"We're…networking." Rayn shuffled as a soft heat rose in his cheeks; he masked his discomfort with a breezy free grin. "And Gineane doesn't care, she's open-minded."

"Okay, Rayn." Voni patted Rayn's shoulder and wandered over to the professor.

"Value's subjective, I guess," Rayn muttered, wiping Voni off his shoulder as he slipped back to the normal people.

Big-mouthed-bigger-muscled comedy-master Wyn was tallying up which of the students at the neighboring table had shared his bed, his voice booming with each exaggerated name as the girls ducked down in embarrassment and pretended not to listen. Voni didn't get the point: yes, Wyn was a sexist brick-brain with an ego, but he was a *funny* sexist brick-brain with an ego. It was okay because it was humorous. Humorous, harmless—and true. It was true! The girl in question with the large assets did look like an ice cream, and it was true, most likely, that Wyn had licked that cone. If the cringing girl really minded, she could speak up.

Rayn swaggered over. "Laying it on a little thick this morning, Wyn?"

"Oh hey boys, check out this lizard," Wyn laughed. "My roommate and *main man,* Rayn Vizzoni. How's our weird little pal doing?"

Rayn shrugged. "Oh, Voni? I dunno. We weren't really talking. He was just there."

"He used to be normal, you know. Then one day he had a bug in his personal program—a ghost in the hallways." Wyn's eyes widened as he lowered his last words into a dramatic whisper. "For a few weeks he completely disappeared, and now—he's like *that.*"

Rayn's insides froze solid. A ghost in the hallways? He struggled to maintain his smirk as the theatrics continued around him. Voni talked in codes, told stories about spirits, and obsessed over the growth of the hallways as if they hadn't always existed. He spent most of his time with people no one else could understand, and rumor had it he descended to the children's levels on a regular basis, as if he reaped some sick enjoyment out of playing with stinking, undeveloped spawn. He even asked his parents to eat with him, as if he desired companionship from the old. Rayn never wanted whatever mental disease Voni had.

Rayn shook himself off with a dry laugh. The story meant nothing. Wyn probably knew a number of pods had flickered out this morning, and he wanted to mess with everyone. Typical Wyn. What a crazy guy.

Two claps from the teacher announced the beginning of class as Voni approached Rayn's table. Wyn grinned and rolled his eyes, twirling a finger by his temple. *Coo-coo...*

Right. It actually wasn't funny anymore.

*To be like Voni...*

"Today we're continuing the cardiac metaphysiology project," said the teacher. "As you already know, the action potential in the heart produces a mechanical rhythm, which then translates to the fluid hydraulics that maintain life. You may *not* know that the concentration of so many electronic signals in one spot, interacting repeatedly over synchronized moments, has atomic implications that affect space-time. Today we will be recording the quark pitch of each of your hearts—the rate at which nearby particles vibrate when the heart beats."

"Bla bla bla," whispered Wyn. "My lunch goes to the guy who comes up with the best pick-up line using this heart machine. 'Baby we might have to calibrate your heartbeat—oh wait, I might have to feel for it'"—Wyn fondled the chest of the guy nearest him, his face as innocent as an empty room, and everyone laughed. Except for Voni. Voni kept his eyes on the pitch-recording device, messing with screws and knobs.

"Hey guys, let's work," he interrupted.

The physical humor continued as they passed the tube around, writing down the readings on its little screen each time it touched a new chest. When they strapped it to Voni, the numbers faded and the machine began to hum.

"ERROR," it read. The young men glanced at each other. They tried again. This time it read a negative number.

Rayn's chest constricted.

*To be like Voni...*

"You got some kind of medical condition?" Wyn grunted.

"I guess it's just who I am." Voni smiled shyly and glanced away.

Rayn trembled.

* * *

The chip-tune music stopped; the sentient stampede rolled back through the square hatches to close themselves in for the night. Deafening chatter sounded as thousands of locks clicked shut all at once. Then, silence—

Except for an odd jostling in the second quadrant of the young adult level.

"I'm gonna kill you!" Rayn bellowed.

"I can't believe you're fighting me over a woman!" Wyn laughed. "Just a woman!"

"She's my girlfriend, you jerk!"

"Apparently not, since, uh, she's in my bed."

Rayn tried to bite back his rage with pragmatism. "Wyn, okay, the hallways are about to lock. Let me in."

"Apologize first."

"Apologize? You made my girlfriend cheat on me!"

"Them's the rules. You can't take a joke, you can't stay with the Wynster."

"Wyn!"

CLICK.

Rayn slammed himself against the hatch with a roar. No one heard. Wall squished over the hatch like a fast-growing fungus. Rayn whirled to dash for another, to ask someone else for help, but with a *slurp* red flesh sealed over each door.

Rayn would be trapped in the hallways until morning.

Oh no. No no no no. Alone—alone, his neurons dying from time spent alone—the silence tormented Rayn's ears. Did skeletal faces bulge beneath the lumps in the slick, smooth surfaces? Did the walls eat people? He'd never felt such darkness, such *throbbing* darkness. The cat-like irises of the many cameras closed into vertical slits, just cuts and texture in skin as the reddish-brown light from the walls dimmed to a mere pulsing glow.

Like the error in his program.

A soft footstep. A heartbeat in his ears.

"No…"

It began to materialize at the end of the hallway, face and hands first. A lithe, glimmering, almost skeletal being flickered towards him, walking in time, one heartbeat after the next.

Rayn puffed himself up. This was not happening. No. He refused. He would scare it away. He could beat everyone in his martial arts section except Wyn. His face heated with a menacing scowl, hiding the chill in his spine.

"Rayn," said the glimmer. Rayn shivered, trying to shake off the voice pouring like soothing liquid into his ears. "Are you ready?" it asked.

"Who are you?"

"I am…Agape." The shimmering mouth paused, head tilted as if just recognizing the fact for the first time. "I am Agape, and I am here to give you what you need."

"I have what I need."

"You need to visit the city."

"This is the *only* city, and I've been everywhere in it."

"No, you have not."

Rayn scoffed. "Try me. Give me a name."

"You call it Synovi."

"Synovi's right here!"

The translucence floated closer, its voice a whisper now. "From your point of view, yes."

Glowing fingertips snatched Rayn's wrist—

Ah! Solid fingers, not at all like the mist they seemed. Rayn twisted away, no longer afraid. These warm hands, like slimy little four-year-old hands, didn't belong to a ghost. Just a starved whippet; a sick child.

"Come!" cried the whippet, then, "Stop!" as Rayn turned to run. He paused at its cry as it threw itself to its knees, and though he'd already crossed the hallway, somehow the creature was beside him yet again, clinging to the edge of his silver robe.

"Please, please—this place is killing you," it whispered.

A panicked pulse fluttered in the arteries of the creature's transparent neck. This was real desperation. Something wet gleamed in the whippet's wide, dark, doe-like stare, and its ribs stilled in frozen breath as it searched his face. What did it know about the hallways that he didn't?

Rayn narrowed his glare, avoiding eye contact as he watched the walls around them. Hellish red images…faces in the goo…

Everything Rayn knew ordered him to curl up in silence and wait for morning.

But if he left the whippet, he would be alone.

Like Voni.

Rayn cleared his throat and borrowed the voice his parents used when they scolded him through the hatches. "I will follow you if you promise to bring me back here."

"You can always come back." Agape sighed, and its feet lifted off the ground as it flew before Rayn to the end of the corridor, taking all the light with it. Darkness closed behind Rayn, and in his imagination the soft walls emitted a sucking sound, absorbing dirt and waste and, if they stood still long enough, *people*, and so he trotted to catch up with the shimmer. Anything to avoid wandering here, lost and solitary, until he came back soft and desperate and eager and stupid like poor Voni.

What was he following, though? Some electromagnetic phenomenon, an AI wrapped in bioenergy, a living inductor that had broken the local programming by proximity? What *was* Agape?

When they reached the back wall, Agape drove a shriveled fist forward, and the entire back wall smashed open.

*?!*

Oxygen streamed out around them into space before Rayn could scream. Agape's soft, clear hand rushed across his nose and mouth; Rayn inhaled in a drowned panic, and fragrance streamed down his throat, through his whole body, as they tumbled out into eternity. The hallway repaired itself with a slurp that faded as the oxygen dissipated.

The city had sealed them out in the void.

He mustn't scream. He mustn't struggle. He mustn't lose his mind. He was suspended in the fragile arms of a beam of light above, or below, or *in* the abyss of scattered dust and stars, and above all he *must not fall*—

Who was he kidding. He was losing it completely.

"My flesh sustains life," Agape whispered before Rayn could begin his panicked kicking. "If you were out here alone, you'd implode from the lack of pressure and oxygen, and flash-freeze."

Yes, thank-you, he knew that. His mile-a-minute heart rate told him that. His heaving, hyperventilating chest told him that. He wanted to vomit.

"But I will protect you. Agape always protects."

Rayn nodded, wide-eyed, as the cool draught continued pouring through his lungs. Adrenaline begged him to struggle. They'd left the tubes—the tubes, all he'd ever known—behind them like roots to a long-dead tree growing in crisscrossing knots and branches through space—

But a terror greater than his fear of the unknown froze his fight. If Agape released him, he died. That was not in the least uncertain. They flew down, around and through the twists of pulsating, living Synovi until a flat planet surface spread below them. They'd gone well below the children's section now, and soon they left the organism city behind altogether. Grey clouds appeared below them, and Rayn shivered.

At least for now he wasn't alone.

# Lower Synovi

Rayn's eyes adjusted to the smog; Agape's darted back and forth, dark irises dilated as it searched for something. The sprite took an experimental breath, nodded to itself, and released Rayn's lungs.

A painful, sharp, face-wrenching sensation ravaged Rayn's nostrils: the place reeked like death and rotten eggs, but since Rayn had never come near either, he had no comparison for the assault. He stifled a weak cough, doubling over as he struggled between the need to breathe and terror of the stench. Shallow breaths, shallow breaths. "What are you looking—"

"Shh!" Agape snarled, baring carnivorous teeth.

Rayn jumped back, hugging himself as Agape continued sniffing the air. Jaws of jagged spikes seemed so much more eerie and terrifying on such a soft, wispy—soft? No, this thing could punch out a wall.

Had it even needed his permission to take him away?

Rayn stamped his feet. Whether it needed his permission or not, it had asked it, and Rayn clung to that small bit of agency, that stupid agreement that made this kind of his own fault, because if this was his fault, perhaps he could fix it.

Fix it? He looked around.

Rectangular structures towered around them. Rayn traced

their height to where the ceiling should be—

The buildings jutted straight up into a vast expanse of gaping grey.

A new cold horror gripped Rayn, dizzying him—he crouched as his chest constricted, his temples pounding with stumbling fear of falling into the bare, hungry abyss above. He'd never been anywhere without a ceiling!

He closed his eyes. No. He had to talk himself into standing. Fear the known, not the unknown: he'd arrived on some kind of planet surface, with gravity always towards the core. He would not fall into the sky. He would not—he would—he—breathe, breathe—

*What if he fell into the sky?*

A small hand rested on his shoulder. Cool fluid flooded his skin like a transdermal endocrine shot, and his heart rate slowed. He stood, an eyebrow raised at the little being as it waved him after it with a somber smile.

"Agape bears all things," it whispered.

Alright then. That was weird, but it felt better. Rayn flexed his shoulder, rolling it and stretching his back as he stepped after Agape. He would escape the sprite when he could, but for now, it seemed he needed it to survive.

A rough pain stopped him in his tracks. He looked down at his bare feet as he stepped forward again, so hurt and confused by this hard ground. The floor did not give way with the same soft, warm, spongy quality he expected from floors, and so he alternated between light tip-toeing and tripping, comforted at least in the knowledge that this couldn't be a nightmare or insanity. He could never dream something so different from what he knew. He picked his way around trash like a toddler learning to walk, thankful that no one he knew could see him now.

"A clawing alarm," Agape whispered. "Screeching alarm!"

"Whu—"

Agape became a whirlwind. It snatched Rayn and slammed him inside a large metal can of refuse. A lid clanged over Rayn. He opened his mouth to cry out—

"Agape." A gravel voice echoed in the alleyway. "You've returned."

Rayn peered through a crack in the lid. From the shadows stepped a deep-jawed, heavy-set man in shimmering black. If Agape seemed too shadowy to be solid, this man seemed too solid to have a shadow, and when Agape whirled, Rayn again heard that spine-numbing snarl.

More shadowless men blocked the other end of the alley, brandishing disembodiment blasters straight out of Rayn's history lessons. His eyes widened—in real life these guns outsized his *legs*.

"I'm warning you, Kohn," Agape said. "You're underarmed."

*Underarmed?* Rayn still feared Agape's teeth enough to consider believing it, but the shadowless leader laughed, black curls bouncing around his face like springs.

"Are we? No, son, we're Regiment IV! I will grant you did amazing things with that dead cat—never saw such a well-improvised bludgeon. But you've shrunk quite a bit since then. This time, you'd best surrender." Kohn paused gravely. "What've you brought back?"

"He did not want to come," Agape said truthfully. "I did not want to force him."

"*Him?*" Kohn guffawed. "*Him?* Hear that, boys? The Ghost now attempts his conspiracy drivel with *men*." The laughter dissolved in a threatening scowl. "Stick to the little girls, Virtu."

Rayn didn't like to think he'd joined the ranks of naïve females, but Agape didn't seem offended. When it replied, the sprite actually sounded bored: "No, Kohn, you know I have to save everyone. This is the only way they'll survive the war."

"The war is over."

Agape sighed. Clearly, it'd said this many times before. "No, Kohn, your Prince will fall, and I don't want him turning off their hearts when he does."

"I cannot imagine a nobler endeavor than for a captain to go down with his ship." Kohn gnashed his teeth. "And if it takes infinite deaths to keep the Prince's heart going, it is absolutely worth it."

Agape sagged. "No, Kohn, that is—as you humans say—'messed up.'"

Kohn grimaced. Agape waited. "You take all the joy out of this debate," Kohn said.

"It's pearls before swine."

"Let's squeal, then." Kohn's biceps rippled. His guns rose to fire.

Agape leapt, spinning, weaving like a needle through fabric around the disembodiment beams criss-crossing the air around him. From behind and before they fired—Rayn sucked in his breath as the creature lit up a rainbow of colors. It dashed between Kohn's legs and disappeared around the corner. The soldiers charged—Rayn saw only belts and guns as they crowded past his refuse can. The roars and wavering buzz of disembodiment cannons continued long after the last soldier rounded the corner.

* * *

Rayn wanted out of the refuse bin *now*, but he waited until his heart rate slowed. No use stumbling into the next surprise pre-panicked. Perhaps the sprite would return?

Did he *want* the sprite to return? Someone wanted him here, but someone else clearly did not, and Rayn was okay with the latter. Better to go home.

Although—Rayn didn't trust Agape's unnatural shadowless enemies any more than he trusted *it,* and he did want to know, if only for safety's sake, what any war in this cesspool could possibly have to do with him. As far as he knew, his danger *began* when he met Agape, but it spoke and acted as if he'd spent his life swallowing plastic bags.

The quiet stink suffocated him. Sound, he needed some kind of sound, something to distract him from the inaudible squelch of bacterial hordes growing over his body. Something sharp dug into his left thigh, and something slimy trickled through his robe where he'd sat down.

Rayn crawled out of the trash can.

The unremarkable man wandered from the narrow alley into a long, wide avenue, searching for some human intelligence, still forcing himself not to cling to the edges of the road to keep from falling into the infinite brown clouds *above—don't even think about above. Focus on the ground.* Rayn began to wonder whether he'd stumbled into some post-holocaust nuclear hazard zone. Papers with images of skeletons and indecipherable ink scratches rippled and snagged past him like tumbleweeds of a bygone era.

The far-off roar of voices grew as he continued down the wide avenue. He hadn't noticed it, at first, but as he walked the sound of his footsteps began to fade under cheers and screams, and his mood improved. Yes! A crowd. From the sound of it, a crowd of normal humans, with normal mass and normal shadows. He could fade in there. For today he'd already spent too much time alone.

A booming voice rose above the din as Rayn broke from the avenue out into a city square boiling with people. Rayn stayed on the edges of the crowd, climbing behind three empty crates just under a broken window.

This voice—oh, there. In the center of the crowd a wooden platform held the booming voice's owner above the masses. A long, gray robe covered the man entirely except for intimidating arm muscles and pale, dead eyes. Rayn ducked down: making eye contact with someone like that could turn you into a Voni.

"People of Synovi," said the dead-eyed man.

His words murdered the noise Rayn loved, and Rayn scowled. In the new dead silence the boomer no longer needed to shout.

He did so anyway. "People of Synovi, I want you to remember your options. You have two, and only two. You may join the Guard to defend the Prince, or you may remain Neutral and work your way to the paradise of Upper Synovi. To those who seek a third option: behold your fate."

The dead-eyed man stepped aside with a flourish. A thin bundle of bones struggled between the two shadowless Guards behind him. At first the creature seemed so small and pale Rayn thought of Agape, and gasped—how had they caught him? With the next blink he realized he saw a starved human being, not living starlight.

The Guards shoved the emaciated thing to the front of the platform and lifted its clothes, showing off bruises, scars, and exposed ribs. The creature—a girl—hacked and fought just to breathe. Her loud wheezes were the only sound that defied the silence: a sick, precious contrast to the death in Rayn's ears.

"Now I shall not ask you to fight your 'Friend.'" The gray dead-eyed man still shouted like a commercial announcer, only now at the girl. "Return to Upper Synovi and fight *us* no more. If you really love this place," he waved his hand in disgust, and bitter laughter echoed across the crowd. "You may stay and help the poor, or whatever you people do, but you mustn't speak of this anti-Prince anymore. Will you go or stay?"

"I will stay." Her voice broke from her throat as from a prison; its volume frightened Rayn, like Agape's snarl in the alleyway.

"And you will fight the Prince no more?"

She laughed, loudly. Eerie happiness echoed against the broken buildings. Her head tilted, low and dangerous, with the grin of a wolf pre-pounce. "Slave," growled the wolf. "Slave, until your eyesight fails and your skin melts from your bones, and even after that, I will never stop fighting. The pitch of my heart won't *let* me stop."

Rayn had no time to react to the bizarre answer.

A gasp choked in his throat—a fist the size of his head slammed into the girl's tiny stomach. Another Guard tripped the wraithlike form. Another stomped on her face.

"Have you changed your mind?"

"No." The voice faded.

Another fist rose.

Rayn whirled to run as the taste of bile clawed up his throat. He stumbled over metal cans and upturned barrels, scrambling back to the wide avenue with his hands over his mouth. His healthy legs picked up pace like pistons rolling one over the other—he ducked into a side passageway and doubled over a trash can, panting. His fingers clenched the metal ridge, knuckles whitening as he dry-heaved.

"Someone has to help her," he choked.

"Why?"

Rayn glanced up, wiping his mouth on his sleeve, too shocked already to run from the lean woman who'd snuck up on him. She stood as tall as he, muscular arms and shoulders bared through a long, black leather dress that swirled around her body to flare out by her boots. She balanced a disembodiment cannon as big as her leg in one hand.

Rayn's eyes fixed on the stranger's weapon. "Somebody has to stop them because—the girl—they're doing things to her," Rayn said.

"She made her own decision. At least allow her the respect of responsibility." The woman turned up her chin, then narrowed her eyes: "You shouldn't be outside dressed like that, upworlder. You will be robbed, and it will be as much your fault as that girl's suffering is hers. Come here."

She turned a small metal object in a hole on a wooden door as tall as Rayn, disengaging some internal latch. It was strange, not ducking to enter a room, but Rayn followed; he couldn't exactly say no to a woman with a gun that big, and he didn't want to stay outside alone.

The building was as hard and cold inside as outside. A jagged metal ramp led "up." Stairs, for someone who'd never dealt with anything remotely similar to height, became another opportunity for humiliation.

Humiliation? No. Rayn would do this right. He watched the woman walk a few steps first. She altered her gait with comfortable grace, swiveling at the hips, and the ramp did not break. Rayn waited until she'd reached halfway, and then jogged to keep himself from looking down through the slats in the metal.

He made it to the top a little winded, but proud. He'd only

ever gone "up" three times in his life: once to leave the warm, pre-programmed organic care of the smallest children's level; once to leave the educable small children for the brawling and natural selection of older youth; and once to leave that hell for the career-bound young adults. Here people went up and down all the time, apparently, and it felt a little dirty. He liked it.

The woman turned another metal bit in another hole to swing open another door, and they entered her empty apartment. She had no shower-tube and no closet, just two or three changes of clothes folded in a bare corner. A long low flat table lay in one end of the room, covered in tapestries with a puff of cloth at one end. Rayn guessed she slept there—this hard floor couldn't cocoon her overnight the way his bedroom floor did.

Rayn stepped past that soft table to the glass window. He could see over the street and the next few buildings, back to the crowded square and the beaten prisoner. His delight with jagged up-ramps and sleeping-tables died fast.

"It's sick that you don't think that's wrong," he muttered.

"It's not about right or wrong. She's with the Invader. The war's an ecosystem: it's not right or wrong when a lion kills a rabbit. It must; that's how it protects itself from starvation. Or, in this case, another lion."

"Invaders?"

"*The* Invader. He claims Synovi belongs to him, and that the Prince's status quo needs to change."

"Seems he's right about that last bit."

"He wouldn't do much better. We would find ourselves dissolved into a hive mind I can't begin to understand. *She* came from Upper Synovi, you know." The woman in black jerked her head towards the window, but didn't look out. She settled on her sleeping-table, legs apart and shoulders square, and wiped a cloth over the gun draped between her legs. "Where you come from. Virtus fly up there to steal your people down here and trick them into using their resources to assist the invasion."

Rayn connected the dots, but kept his mouth shut about Agape: she spat 'Virtu' like a filthy word, eyes blazing and nose wrinkled.

"Did the Virtu make her do something—wrong?" he asked. "Like a war crime?"

"Again, it isn't about right and wrong. Perhaps you have that luxury where you come from, but here it's ecology. I don't like how the Prince forces his way on people, but I understand him. It's survival of the fittest, and we just have to be more fit."

Rayn fidgeted as the woman gazed at her reflection in the black barrel of her cannon; finally, she spoke again, as if to justify something. "It's just that the Invader doesn't behave in a way that makes sense. Gibberish follows his ethics. He 'brings perfect peace' but 'promises a sword of division'—it's phrases like that, and the strange faculties of illogic that possess his people, that make me prefer the lion I know to the Leviathan I don't.

"Anyway." She rose. "He's just another chess-player against the Prince. The Guards, the Virtus, and rebels like Sishana out there—they're pawns. I will not be a pawn. I'm Neutral."

She fixed her eyes hard on his, for emphasis. Rayn wanted for a second to avert his gaze, but he did not. He would not look weak.

"How do you know about my world?" he asked.

"We all hear rumors from those the Virtus bring down here. A living network of tunnels that feeds your every need?" She whistled with envy. "I'm working my way there. There are connections, if you're able to pay, and pass certain tests—it's a black market of sorts. You wouldn't believe how many different groups offer upper-life investment strategies; there are many paths to paradise."

"I wouldn't believe it, no. I've never seen that happen before. And if it were common, I'd have heard about…this place."

Her eyes flickered with darkness for a moment—despair, or doubt?—but she played a sneaky smile over it and leaned on her cannon. "I doubt any of us who make it up there would talk about our origins with people who see upward mobility as a thrice-in-a-lifetime privilege."

"It's seven times, actually."

"Well, you'd never notice if I made it. I'd just appear in the hallways one day." The smile faded. "You got down here somehow. Are you with them?"

"The Invaders? No, I'm—I'm Neutral I guess." He glanced back out the window. His gut tightened and he felt dizzy. This was happening. They were standing here talking about her plans for the future while *that* happened outside.

The girl in black watched his gaze and sighed. "You don't understand what it's like down here. The best way to help her is to stay out of her way and honor her decision. Guards become angry when more Invaders pop up, and they'd only degrade her more, to break you. You see," she stepped over to lean on the wall next to the window, across from him, "if everyone would stay out of each other's business—just live and let live—you'd see a completely different world here. Like yours."

"Economically, maybe," Rayn said. "But socially—"

"Look, this isn't politics. This is the philosophy of survival. Wait—" The lady's eyes popped out the window. "Whoa!"

Rayn held his breath—he recognized the glowing sprite that dashed over the platform, smashed one Guard to the ground with one puny hand, bowled another off the stage with a tiny kick, tripped the gray man, spat in his face—Rayn held back a cheer.

Agape snatched the ragged mess of broken humanity off the platform, and with what looked like a passionate kiss, disappeared with her over the city.

Wait—wait, Rayn needed that ride home!

Rayn cried out and dashed back outside and down. The woman chased him to the top of the stairs. "Wait, you're still dressed like a walking moneybag! You need to change, you—you, what's-your-name!"

"Rayn!" he yelled up, pausing under the balcony. "What's yours?"

"Nina! Where do you think you're going, Rayn?"

"Home!"

# Prison

ayn found his way to a large warehouse that was unremarkable amongst the other filthy buildings squatting along the dock. He heard Agape whisper to the tattered girl about "the throne-room."

"That's ominous," Rayn muttered. He decided not to follow too closely; instead he crept around the outside towards the back end of the building. He saw a window, high up on the wall, and had no trouble climbing the debris and discarded barrels piled under it. From this height he could look in and see the whole warehouse, except for a dark patch just under him.

The enormous front door creaked open just a crack, and Agape floated in, carrying the shattered human girl.

"Well done." Low, voiceless words echoed from the dark patch within the warehouse. They seemed to enter Rayn's head before entering his ears. "I rescued two from the South execution blocks while you were gone."

Agape gasped. "I thought they were too far gone!"

"And you thought the Western prisoners could only be saved with magic, but I sent a child, and that worked much better." The Words laughed. "You have a lot to learn. And yet you trust. Agape always trusts."

Rayn saw the shadow of a hand laid on Agape's shoulder.

Fingertips strayed down to brush the side of what had been the emaciated girl's face: Rayn saw no features, only blood over a gaping hole of a mouth, as hands lifted the crushed girl into the shadows. Rayn grimaced, gripping his stomach. He heard a deep heartbeat, a thump that echoed through the wall to vibrate the trash pile where he stood, as if when the shadows cradled the girl to a warm chest Rayn felt her comfort. "Oh Beloved," said the Words. "You've been through so much for me."

"You went through more for me," she croaked. Rayn recognized a smile now, one that turned on the sprite huddled at a distance as a great lady beamed upon her page. "And thanks to Agape's breath I'm still alive."

"Yes. But your work is done here. Come home with me."

"I would like that, Beloved…I'd like to see a real sun for the first time, you know."

"You will." A face rubbed against the bloody smile, caressing her like a mother cat nudges her kittens. The girl began to light up—literally light up, with blinding colors exploding down vivid chocolate arms and legs, bright blue eyes and jet black hair—and the blood on her body suddenly became elaborate crimson warpaint. A terrifying glory blasted from her for a second—Rayn shielded his eyes—

When he looked back she was gone.

*What the hell on earth?*

"Did you turn her into a star, or was that what she always was?" Agape asked.

"She turned into starlight a long time ago, when she first loved me back," the Words said. "I only had to bring it out over time."

"The Guards never knew what they were dealing with, did they."

"No one ever does."

*No one ever does.*

A vibrating, like instruments in Rayn's thorax screaming above the sound of an orchestra of broken glass out of tune—!

Rayn's fingers dug into his pecs as if he could choke his heart into normality. What! What was this tangling din, like the sound of a crash, but extended, and compounded into a *feeling*, into confusion and conflict and crashing—?

Rayn slid down the pile of debris, gripping his chest.

Where did the girl go? Did the shadow-thing absorb her? She seemed alright with it, so most likely not, but what a terrifying female! He almost dared to like her better crushed and destroyed. Her full potential, her power, that violent light in her eyes, all *freaked him out*. If a being like that even touched you you'd go insane.

He suddenly remembered Voni.

But agh, his heart, his heart! Rayn coughed to breathe. This tightening, this fluttering, this guilt married to desire and terror—he was sick. It was that thing, making him sick. Perhaps it radiated something…radioactive. Or he was allergic to that kind of animal. Either way, Rayn stumbled through the trash pile, tripping and tumbling to get away from the window of weirdness.

He'd just hit the street corner when suddenly the flipping cacophony in his chest stopped.

Ba-dum, ba-dum, the warm normal *regularness* of his heart-beat returned, as if—the buzzing left? The pitch resolved? His rhythm hadn't changed at all, but whatever it was, he felt better as a warm shadow passed by him, and almost without thinking he stepped forward to follow the cloaked figure from which the safeness emanated.

But the figure was rounding the block back toward the front door of the warehouse.

Rayn cursed. He wouldn't go back to that weird window. He stepped out of the shadow.

The stretching and pulsing in his chest returned, like he had a cat and a dog killing each other in there. He was forced back into the shade. For argument's sake, he tried to step out again—no, no that hurt. In this cloaked figure's shadow he'd found the only relief from his new—his new radiation injury—whether he wanted it or not.

Rayn followed the figure for now, crouching behind rubble and clinging to the corners and walls, hating every step that took him closer to the warehouse door. He should leave. He should just leave. He didn't like the way the figure walked. Rats scurried away from its reflection in the puddles; cockroaches poured out of hidden crannies as if to flee an invisible pesticide. And how did such a normal-sized person have a shadow so wide, and broad?

At last the figure reached the warehouse door. It stood for a moment, head bowed, as if steeling itself. Its shoulders heaved in a deep breath…

Then it puffed out its chest and hurled both wall-sized doors wide open.

"Invader," boomed the hooded figure. "Let me have my world!"

Light congealed from all the cracks and windows to condense down into a visible being, like gas to water becoming ice. The Invader's ice lips parted and light flickered from his mouth with his breath.

"Your food ration," scoffed the hooded figure, reaching into his sleeve and hurling a bag at the Invader's feet. "To remind you that I am above you. I provide for you. You pretend I do not, that you do not *need* me, that we are not each other's Yin and Yang, but I see you, saving up those cookies in the corner like a hamster hoarding grain. What are you saving them for?"

Rayn poked his head around the door-jam to see the careful pile of biscuits arranged on top of a crate. The Invader lifted the new bag in silence, inspected each item, and added two cookies to his arrangement.

"Why do you not answer me?" The shadow figure threw back its cloak and marched across the room. Rayn's eyes couldn't focus on what it was—it seemed to jump-cut between steps, like a broken film, growing larger between each still until it towered above the Invader, stretched out, fuzzy and pixelated, like a photo expanded beyond its base resolution, blown up beyond what it actually was.

"Even now, you ignore me?" it whispered.

The Invader did not look up to the pixelated face towering above him; his ice eyes pierced the giant's body to meet Rayn cowering in the doorway. Rayn's chest ached again. He wanted to hide, but he could not move. "You know what you must do to be cured," said the Words.

"You said my wound was incurable," hissed the blown-up image.

"Hm? Oh, yours is, yes. But I can do anything."

"I tire of your oxymorons, old thing. I am the Prince! My world and I need no curing. Come. Let me remind you of your chains!"

With the Prince's triumphant order, the Invader sighed and closed his eyes, wincing as he turned to bare his back to his enemy. For a moment he waited there, his head bowed, as he knelt on the worn spot on the floor where Rayn suspected he knelt every day. The Prince's eyes glittered with expectant hunger.

The Prince twisted the Invader's wrist behind his back and dug claws into his spine.

A rift in space, in time, surged around their connection. The world around the two rippled and faded; they became the only reality from the dawn of time. A series of scenes overlaid over the same instant: in the shadows of a dying garden of olive trees the Invader groaned, shoulders heaving as the Prince turned his back on an age-old friendship; in the frigid light of an iron mountaintop the Invader writhed, his wrists straining against shackles and his bare back pressed against frozen stone, teeth clenched to hold back a scream as the Prince, an eagle, buried its beak into an open wound in the Invader's side, digging around with hook and claws to rip off a chunk of liver; the Invader smiled through sweat and agony as a bullet impacted his chest, and as he fell Rayn saw the Prince holding the gun, and for an odd second Rayn seemed to feel eye contact, as if the Invader had taken the bullet for *him*.

How long the torture continued Rayn didn't know. The moments were eternal in something other than longitudinal time—like sideways eternal instead of forward eternal? At last the Invader straightened, untwisted himself, and drew back his hand; the rift closed, and he stood cradling a burnt wrist over a Prince curled in slobbering satisfaction on the floor. The excess blown-up mass puddled around the Prince, leaving him a bit smaller than his original, human-like size, and he shuddered in the liquid like a newborn in its mother's blood and urine.

"He'll be in a trance for a while," said the Invader, to Rayn. "You can come in now."

Rayn was too flabbergasted to know what to feel, and in that empty space lived only logic. "Why don't you—" Rayn drew his finger across his throat. If *his* enemy lay vulnerable on the floor, after that, he'd kill him for sure.

"If he dies, so does everyone connected to his heart," said the Invader. He waited for a moment, *you can come in now* still hanging between them on the air. When Rayn didn't enter, the Invader lifted his plate of cookies and walked toward Rayn. "I've been saving these for you."

"You don't know me." Rayn wanted to dash away, but that would force him outside the Prince's now much smaller shadow.

"I know the hallways locked on you almost six hours ago, and you must be hungry by now."

"But he said that's like a month of your food. You can't have saved it for something that happened by chance."

"I can't spend a month looking forward to my meeting with Rayn Vizzoni?"

"But I didn't know about this meeting."

"You didn't need to know. You're not the one who needed to save up cookies."

Something within Rayn wanted to challenge the Invader, to call him a liar, but the light streaming from the being's transparent nostrils distracted him and made the whole accusation absurd. Rayn had never seen a child present a crayon drawing to its mother, or he would've recognized the eager joy on the Invader's face.

It was weird.

How could he get out of this?

"You can take a cookie and run. It's okay. You should come back, though, before your chest stops hurting," said the Invader. "It'll stop hurting soon."

"Why? Why does it hurt?"

"Because you're getting better.  In any sickness, the point where you're unconscious, or in a coma, or drowsy—the point where you no longer *feel* ill—that point means death. You're coming out of that. You're feeling."

"So you made me sick."

"No, I made you *feel* sick. Your heart's *been* sick for a while. You're feeding the Prince and feeding on him, and when I do kill him, you'll die, too, if we don't break you free."

"Hearts don't feed. They pump blood."

The Invader tilted his head, as if thinking about something else. He poured the cookies into a bag that materialized from nowhere before responding. "You don't remember your cardiac metaphysiology project, from the beginning of this journey?"

"No…"

"Try and remember it."  The Invader tied the cookie bag around Rayn's wrist in a large loop, as if afraid to touch Rayn's skin. "You need to leave before he wakes up."

Rayn hesitated, looking down at the shadow he didn't want to leave. The buzzing in his chest had felt awful, but he couldn't just follow this pixelated being around for who knew how long until it wore off.  Especially not if this being could torture and—but maybe the Invader deserved it? Or—

Rayn saw the Prince stir, and his legs decided for him. He ran.

# Woman

Rayn collided with Nina back in the large wide avenue. "What the hell is wrong with this place?" he cried out, his breath heavy with chest pain.

"What happened to *you*, Upworlder?"

"I—I don't know!"

He gripped her biceps, teeth gritted as his eyes squeezed shut, focused on textured leather and warm muscle. Something real. Not blinding, ethereal, or weird—and not solid and shadowless, like a grim brown sky to fall into, or a gruesome example-execution. Something *Neutral*.

His palms were sweating against her arms.

"Gah," he leapt back. "I'm sorry. I don't—I don't—"

Her fingers tapped near the trigger of the disembodiment blaster almost her height.

Rayn panicked. "I'm so sorry, I shouldn't have touched you, I don't—"

"Don't normally run down the street and grab women you hardly know?" Her eyes teased.

Relief rushed into Rayn's face—then, complicated embarrassment, as Nina's voice lowered with a soft patience he couldn't imagine from someone with a gun that large. "It must be so shocking for you to be here," she said. "Like a baby newly born.

I would cry, I think."

Rayn regained himself and smirked. "A new baby—that's not exactly the way I'd like to think of myself."

Nina chuckled. The gentleness hung around her for just one second more as she lowered her eyes, brushed her hair behind her ear—and then hoisted her gun back over her shoulder. Authority returned. "I bet you're hungry. Would you like to head back to my place?"

"Sure!" Rayn squeaked as his eyes fixed on the gun again. He coughed, reining in his enthusiasm to try again. "Sure," he said in a deeper voice.

"I don't suppose you…cook?" she asked. "I heard Upper Synovians sometimes take classes."

"Yeah, actually," he smiled, happy to finally find something he wasn't clueless about. "I'm pretty good. Lemme see what you have, and I'll make magic. And—I have cookies."

He didn't disappoint. She didn't have much of a kitchen—just a box of foodstuffs and a portable electrical stove—but Rayn found something similar to eggs and formed the beginnings of a stir-fry. He added onions and tomatoes and separately started creaming her canned spinach. Soon the stench of city retreated from her apartment, and Rayn could inhale.

"Wow. That certainly smells flavorsome," Nina said.

"Flavorsome? I guess so," he laughed.

"What?"

"You use words that seem too fancy for your tone, out of place. That's all."

She sat back on the cot, picked up a rag, and began polishing her disembodiment blaster. "If we're going to talk about out of place, we should talk about you," she said.

"That sounds ten times more ominous when you're shining

your gun."

"Ah, yes. There are no weapons up there, I hear."

"That's not—no, weapons exist, I think. Wejust don't swing 'em all over the place like you do. There are safety classes—psych evals—licenses."

She laughed. "Safety classes? It's a gun, it's not meant to be safe."

"Anyway," Rayn muttered, gazing into the sizzling eggs. "Who I am isn't where I come from. I don't really like my job, or my friends, or anything except the city's anthem."

"I wish I could live there."

"I know. But it's not—not like you think. It is, and it isn't. I dunno. Don't get me wrong, I want to go home, but there's no one—no one there has any real—we're not real up there."

"What do you mean?"

"I don't know." But Rayn brightened, waving her over. "Come eat!"

She crept over and crouched beside him, glancing from the creamed spinach to the stir-fry. "You are—going to have to bear with my ignorance," she said. "There are these complicated feasts in stories, but in real life I don't have the luxury of wastingfood on experiments that might fail. I eat straight from the can or straight off the plant; I know nothing of combining ingredients."

Her admission made him laugh, not *at* her, but because it felt *joyous* to show her something new. He took the long stickpins out of her hair and washed them in her sink. "Chopsticks," he said.

"Okay. We do that, too."

"Open up."

She glanced at him, then at the steaming portion on the

chopsticks, then back at him.

"Open your mouth," he smiled.

She did, pursing her eyes shut and wrinkling her nose. He let the food slide past her lips and waited. She peeked with one eye, then the other, as she chewed. "Savory, with the crunch, and the acid together—that's an excellent idea, actually," she said finally, mouth still full. "Hmm. My goodness."

Rayn's chest warmed inside; he squirmed a little, smiling. His girlfriend—well, ex-girlfriend—always cooked better than he did, so he could never show her anything for fear of criticism. He startled a bit when he realized he'd compared Nina to—to *her*, but he ignored himself and focused on not spilling food all over the woman in black leather.

Nina laughed—"your turn," she said, and took the chopsticks. Rayn opened his mouth.

She dropped egg and onion all over his shirt. "Oh, sorry!" she gasped, fingers darting to pick up the mess. "Are you okay?"

"Uh, yeah," he said.

"Oh, yes—of course you're okay. It's just food." She laughed. "Stupid me."

She glanced at him, and at the half-empty pan, and retreated back to the cot and her gun with her eyes lowered. She didn't say anything for a bit. Rayn shoveled his portion into his mouth, then rose with a sigh to carry the pan and can of spinach over to the sink.

He wondered, as he cleaned up, what he'd done. Perhaps he was imposing on her. He didn't know what else to do with himself, though. Even wondering what to do next doubled his stomach over in unsettled panic. Nina seemed to be the only halfway normal person he'd interacted with so far. That had to account for the weird tickling under his cheeks.

Unless—the corner of his mouth lifted—he felt this because he liked her.

Which he wouldn't fight if he did.

"I'm not holding you up from your schedule or something, am I?" he asked.

She smirked. "My schedule? No. I'm—I am not usually like this, you know."

"Like what?"

"Giggly and awkward."

"You don't giggle. You've got a pretty laugh," he said.

"See, and I'm never insecure. I don't require your affirmation of my laugh."

"That's—well, okay then." Rayn looked away from her, back towards the dishes.

"I—appreciate—your affirmation of my laugh, though," she said.

"Well okay then." Rayn smiled to himself. He heard her footstep, and soon felt her standing right next to him.

"Let me help with my own cleaning," she said.

"I would, but it's done. What do you normally do now?"

"Well, I normally look for work. I'm a bodyguard or bouncer for whoever needs it."

He nodded, raising his eyebrows. "Cool, cool. What do you do for fun?"

"I read. I've collected a lot of books. Would you like to see?" She smiled, a broad smile with sparkling eyes, and pulled a box out from under her cot. From the box she pulled several rectangles of tightly bound paper with more little skeletal scratches on them.

"Someone's really bad at drawing," said Rayn.

"That's not drawing. That's writing."

"No—writing is when you record something to a disc, like for your personal academic program."

"I have no idea what you just said, but this is writing. It tells a story."

He narrowed his eyes, trying to gauge from her face whether or not she was serious. "How can it tell a story if you can't interface with it?"

Her eyes lit up. "Come," she said. "Sit next to me here, and I'll read to you."

She settled on her cot and he sat next to her, keenly aware of the giant gun touching his thigh, separating them. He leaned in towards the paper, listening as she ran her finger across the page, under the scratches, and told him a story. Some of the scratches repeated with the sounds she made. She said "the," and two tree-looking figures came up every time. He sucked in his breath, and his eyes widened—he got it.

"It's a code," he interrupted.

"It is. Do you like the story?"

"This is really cool." He gazed at her in admiration. "Thanks for showing me!"

"You aren't even a third of the way down the first page yet. Thank me when it ends."

And so she read.

Rayn did not understand the passing of time without the chip-tune music that normally told him what to do, and the light never changed beyond the grey-brown of lower Synovi's ugly sky, so he never knew if they spent weeks or only days together. It didn't matter. They read all her books; he even began to distinguish the letters for himself. She loved the fantasy stories, but Rayn loved her *real* books: textbooks, a dictionary, an encyclopedia, things that brought foreign places and creatures in front of him. Nina didn't like to read those for fun, she said, but she didn't mind reading those with him.

Every now and then Rayn would wander over to the window, gaze out across the square, and wonder when he should chase down Agape for a ride home. He didn't dare tell Nina that something about Agape intrigued him, and he couldn't erase the goddess-martyr from his mind. He wanted to ask how it felt to transform like that—and whether it was worth the cost she'd paid.

He also wondered how much he actually wanted to go home right now, with this whole question about heart sickness, and the Prince, and the Invader. His chest ached and buzzed when he thought about it.

Nina intrigued Rayn, too, but in a more solid, less wandering way. He wanted to explore her thoughts, memorize the flex of her muscles when she hoisted her gun onto her shoulder, bathe in her voice, stroke the side of her face, pull her body in against his and memorize those curves with his eyes shut—but he didn't touch her.

It was such a different feeling. With his ex he'd just wanted to joke and have sex, and maybe, if she had something *worth* hearing, something that applied to his life or career in some useful way, he'd talk. That wasn't often.

With Nina he suddenly didn't care about "worth"; he worried *he* wasn't adding enough value to *her*. Perhaps, he admitted in a moment of softness, in some way he'd pushed his ex over to Wyn—treating Gineane like she had to perform to interest him. Perhaps she'd been a worthwhile person in her own right, like Nina, and he'd missed out.

But he wasn't about to miss out now. When Nina grew hungry, he delighted her with his cooking; when she grew sleepy, he curled up on her floor and listened to her slow breaths. She became his chip-tune anthem, and he became jealous of that gun—always cradled in her sleeping arms, always repaired and polished under precise, loving hands, always touching her back or thigh, always protecting her.

But one day—or hour, or week—she put the cannon on the floor while they read. That day, she leaned against Rayn, her warm back against his chest as he breathed, and sighed.

# Door Unlocked

Rayn noticed *time* again when he ran out of biscuits.

He was practicing his writing when he finished off the last one. He'd developed a habit of venturing out into the streets just outside the apartment to collect the pamphlets tossed around by the non-Neutrals, and on the back, in the blank spaces, he'd begun scratching recipes for Nina to keep. He couldn't make her a recipe book, really, but he could make her a recipe—pile—of some sort, and that was something.

He did this so his brain wouldn't atrophy when she left him alone.

Rayn glanced outside at the grey clouds. Usually she came back from her bodyguard gigs after about the time it took him to write out three recipes and eat two biscuits. She was late.

Rayn paced. He'd gone through the whole bag of cookies? What did that mean? How much time had he spent here, mucking around this stranger's apartment in—in some kind of trance? Waiting for what? For Agape to come back and push him on the next step of this weird journey? Or for the hallways to change and direct him homeward? Nina still had not found an agency she could afford to take her to Upper Synovi, and like Rayn she did not trust anyone who offered to take her for cheap. So she kept working, and he kept waiting, and...why had he not left already?

Because the silent, periodic vibration in his chest frightened him, so he feared returning home with it, but he feared asking the Invader and the Prince about it more?

No, see, that was exactly the type of wishy-washy woo-woo thought that came to people without schedules, constant connectivity, and a chip-tune anthem to keep them on track. It had begun. The aloneness had begun melting his neurons.

With no more recipes and biscuits to keep him occupied, Rayn swore he'd go insane, so he closed up the apartment behind him and—

Should he lock the door?

He had seen Nina do it.

He didn't want to lock himself out. Look what had happened last time a door locked on him. The red hallways—

The red hallways were gone. Here, no one took you where you needed to go. Here you decided where you needed to go, and you walked there on your own. No safety, no ceiling, only infinite gray sky.

Rayn trembled. He wanted to lock the door. To make the first real unilateral decision in his life. Locking the door meant embracing the risk of not turning back. It meant trusting that Nina would open up for him again when he returned.

It meant he'd keep her books safe. Of course he would lock the door. Of course, in this kind of world only a fool would not lock the door!

Rayn did not lock the door.

Halfway down the stairs he turned to look at the closed door. A closed door looked like a locked door. Who would want to steal from Nina, anyway? She was Neutral. If Rayn needed to run somewhere and hide, he needed to run here and find a door he could hide behind. An unlocked door meant a contingency plan.

He'd only be gone for a little while.

* * *

It did not occur to Rayn until far too late that without hallways to direct you where you needed to go, you needed to actually *know* the locations of things.

He did not know the location of the warehouse where he could ask for more information about his heart. Or get more biscuits. Or just see, one more time, and come to terms with the existence of the strangeness of the being he didn't really want to think about.

At first, the feeling of lostness only frustrated him. This stupid city, right? The streets were dysfunctional. Stupid. Trash everywhere. Look at that rat. They were supposed to be extinct. Time to go back. Not a good investment of his precious time. As a law student, he knew better than to waste time.

Rayn turned around, and looked at the grey sky, and the dull streets, and the turns, all alike…

He also did not know the way to Nina's apartment.

Rayn's stomach gurgled, right on cue.

The hell? Now his stomach, too? Would every organ in his body fall apart? Why—what—this *pinching* in his belly terrified him. The ache stretched up through his throat to leave a dry, rancid taste in his mouth like acid and rot.

Now Rayn's heart-rate rose simply out of fear. This felt a million times worse than the heart vibrations. This felt like death. His body wanted something. What? What did it want?

Rayn contemplated putting a bread-crust from the refuse bin

into his mouth.

Why? What?

The realization almost swept him off his already-dizzy feet—was this *hunger*?

The chiptune anthem ensured everyone ate small, perfect amounts at small, perfect intervals. With the biscuits by his side, Rayn had unconsciously kept to those small five-to-six-times-a-day meals, and he ate more for pleasure than for need. This true need—no one should ever feel this!

The city's inhabitants should know what to do about this.

Rayn ran from the feeling, peering around corners until he found people. A gaggle of Guards leaned on chairs and dumpsters and walls around an open door. Some of them rummaged around inside, passing books and cups and other random things from the doorway to the group outside. Perhaps some kind of refuse collection group or something.

"Excuse me," Rayn said.

"What for?" None of the Guards looked up from their quiet exchanges except for the one built like Wyn, with the neck-scruff.

"Excuse me?" Rayn didn't understand the response.

"I said, what for? What you wanna get excused for? What you did?"

"Oh—oh, nothing, I—"

"Look, little man, you got a confession or not? I'm busy cleanin' shop and huntin' Traitors, so unless you're gonna be worth the time we ain't talking. Got that?"

Rayn scowled. *He* wasn't worth the time?

"You know, he walks weird," another Guard pointed out. "Maybe his pocket's worth your time, Smurl."

Smurl smirked. "He ain't wearing Upper Synovi clothes

though."

"You never know. Maybe he made a friend. Those clothes are pretty clean, could be he knows a woman."

Rayn raised both of his hands in feigned surrender, thankful now for the itching rustle of the ragged carpet-like shirt and pants Nina lent him. "I like to be clean. Prevents disease. Can you direct me to—to—an apartment?"

"An apartment?" Smurl tilted his head. His lower lip curled over the top of his mouth as if his teeth needed to meet his nose. "You trying to be funny, little man?"

"No, I—" Rayn stopped. All around him lay apartments. He had no idea how to distinguish Nina's street. "It's an apartment with stairs, and a brown door." Everything in Lower Synovi looked brown. "Not this color brown, like a red-brown."

Two or three Guards now stopped their chore to stand up behind Smurl. "We should kill him."

"Wait, what?"

"You're wasting Guard time," said Smurl.

"I'm not—" Rayn's lips fluttered. He had no way of returning to Nina's apartment, and he imagined the hunger now as a parasite clawing away at his temples and blurring his vision. Lost—was that the word for the panic surging in his closing throat?

"A warehouse? Can you direct me to a warehouse?"

"There's a Warehouse District, yeah. Why should I direct you there?"

"Because you'll feel better sending me there, than killing me and cleaning up a mess?"

"It's not me that's gotta clean up." Smurl unbuckled his disembodiment blaster. The rest of his soldiers followed his lead, stepping forward as one fluid predator.

Rayn panicked. "Look, my heart's feeding the Prince, right? You don't want him to have one less heart, do you?"

Smurl froze mid-swagger. The other Guards looked at him questioningly as he crossed the distance between himself and Rayn and lowered his voice. "Hey now, whaddyou know about that? You ain't no Guard."

"I…overheard, I…I saw the Prince."

Smurl's sticky fist jammed up under Rayn's chin, clutching the collar of his itchy shirt. "Now listen here, no one sees the Prince. He's invisible."

"He is?"

One of the Guards back behind Smurl set down the bookshelf he was carrying. "Hey, Smurl, what's he talking about, about the Prince's heart?"

"Shaddup you, it's an upper-level thing," Smurl yelled back.

"How does *he* know about it?"

Smurl looked Rayn up and down, eyes narrowed, scruffy lower mandible protruding like a tumor. "Yeah. How do you know? You been spying?"

"I just…saw the Prince." Rayn gulped.

"Well let's see about that. You wanna go down to the Warehouse District? We'll take you down to the Warehouse District."

Smurl began to walk, without any ceremony and without releasing Rayn's collar. In that manner, dragged down the street by an oversized oaf, Rayn found the warehouse he was seeking.

* * *

"Prince, sir? Someone to see you. I think he's an overlander, spying on you."

Rayn stood panting by the door of the warehouse, trying to get a little more distance between his neck and his collar still tightened in Smurl's sweaty grip. Two other Guards stood behind them, following Smurl's eyeline to stare just to the right of where the vague cloaked figure was exiting the Invader's prison, trailing an enormous shadow.

The Prince paused in the doorway. "Hello again," he said.

"He's been talking about your heart," Smurl accused.

Rayn could see over the Prince's shoulder to where the Invader cocked his head. The Prince leered back to nod at the Invader, eyebrow raised, before turning his hooded visage back to Rayn.

"How kind of you to take concern for my well-being," he murmured.

"I—I just want to go home," Rayn said.

"Oh, you poor boy." The Prince clucked like a hen, pacing around Rayn. The shadow cooled Rayn's chest with a surprising relief that tasted of citrus. "Isn't it unfair," the Prince clucked. "What *he* does to you?" An accusing arm pointing to the mysterious ice-thing hovering like a dust-cloud in the darkness. "Isn't it unfair that he claims to care about you, only to kidnap you from your safety and force you to change the hearts with which you were born?" Hissing grew to a shout. "That he forces his way on others, instead of changing himself?"

"My Being holds your Universe in the balance. I cannot change," the Invader thundered.

"So you claim!" The Prince whirled, and a long arm or tendril shot out past Rayn. He gripped a Guard and thrust the squirming man towards the Invader, stalking forward.

The Guard gripped his chest, groaning. "Sir...sir!"

"Do you care about all of them?" The Prince jeered, nearing

the edge of the Invader's cloud as the Guard's groans became a scream. "Even this one?"

"Stop!" The Invader cried.

"You stop." The Prince hurled the Guard into the Invader, and as flesh hit energy field the man exploded. Blood and intestine splattered across the warehouse.

The Guard's heart tumbled to the floor by Rayn's feet, and dissolved into ash.

"Brother!" another Guard screamed and rushed the Invader, his disembodiment blaster firing on repeat.

"No, listen!" The Invader roared with the edge of a sob in his voice. "Your heart's not right—you'll die if we touch!"

"Your threats mean nothing! We will never submit to you!" The Guard rushed into the glow with tears running down his face.

He fell to the floor at the edge of the cloud, clutching his chest—dead.

Rayn's tongue felt dry and sticky with panicked breaths. He had been just centimeters from the Invader when the Being gave him cookies. He could have died, too! He shut his mouth, fists clenched, trying to process.

"I told you all never to follow me here," the Prince muttered.

"We need to be close to you, my Lord," Smurl croaked. "We need you."

"We need you," the others repeated, kneeling in his shadow.

The pixels around the Prince smiled; the hood nodded to the Invader again, gloating.

The Prince turned to Rayn. "If you kneel, too, you can help us fight this evil that would force us to change. You can find contentment, right where you are."

Rayn gazed around him at the soldiers, some almost licking

the Prince's shade. This groveling bothered him.

"I want to be Neutral," Rayn said hoarsely. "I can't—I can't fight the battles you two have here—I'm from Upper Synovi—I just need to go home!"

Smurl looked up with a snarl. "So you're too good for us, Upworlder?"

"No, Smurl." The Prince patted Smurl's shorn head. The Guard almost purred like a cat. "We will tolerate neutrality." He glanced behind him, and waved at his Guards to follow him out. "But the Invader will not."

Rayn felt those words as a threat when red eyes glittered at him from under the hood—before he could respond, the Prince was gone, and the gnawing cacophonous pain returned to his chest.

# Nina

Rayn stood there in the dark, his heart and stomach and brain aching all at once. A shimmering luminescence peaked its head out from behind a stack of boxes, and he saw the familiar Virtu that had brought him into this war.

"Let us go to her," it said.

So Rayn walked back to Nina's apartment guided by Agape. He did not speak for most of the journey, and he still could not tell one twisted brown grime-lined street from another.

His belly churned rocks and ground wood with violent yearning.

"You know he cares about you, yes," Agape said presently. Gusts of putrid nuclear wind seemed to poke holes in its flimsy body.

"I don't really know anything right now," Rayn answered. In his annoyed hunger he found himself enjoying it a little bit when his words made the sprite visibly deflate like a squeezed-out plastic bag.

"Do you not feel the pounding in your chest?" it asked.

"That started when I met the Invader."

"No, your ability to *notice* it started when you met him."

"I don't think I've been walking around having mini-heart attacks all my life," Rayn said. "But we could go back and forth like this all day. I'm studying to be a lawyer—what's your *evidence* that we all need this heart transplant thing?"

Agape fluttered above his head, then down on his left, then around him in circles as it thought. "You can't travel forward in time fast enough to see the proof of something that happens in the future, and nothing like this has ever happened before. So I suppose it's like with global warming. Do you remember global warming, from your history classes?"

"So yeah, like I guess graphs of things getting worse would be evidence for some future catastrophe," Rayn nodded.

"So the worsening chest pain, the emptiness in your life, the slavishness of the Guards as they get closer to the Prince, the heartlessness in both our societies—is that proof that the world needs change?"

"You're listing unrelated things, and you could attribute their causes to almost anything." Rayn anticipated the sprite's next thought: "I guess you could say that's like attributing the many signs of global warming to many causes, but we use correlation graphs for that—we can see when different events increase certain measurements."

"If you stay long enough, you will see that the unkindnesses and their emptiness decrease when you get closer to the Invader," Agape offered.

"I haven't seen that, though. I've seen people implode when they get close to him. Apparently through no fault of his own, but still. I get that it's because the polarity of their hearts is still 'off,' but I haven't seen evidence that we need that proximity for any kind of goodness. Bravery, I guess, I've seen with the starlight martyr, but I didn't understand that."

"Bravery is the height of every virtue anyway," Agape said. "It allows her, and others, to save others by sharing the cure even if the consequences are severe. Charity is a side effect of that care."

"So his people have never, ever done anything wrong?" Rayn raised an eyebrow.

"No, but now that's like measuring an antibiotic against a really horrible disease. Sometimes it takes a while for the cure to work."

"Basically, it seems like I can only really prove I need this transplant by dying without it," Rayn said.

"Well I mean, don't you usually measure your medicines by whether or not your symptoms start to go away? Do you really need to wait until the last minute to know something works?"

Rayn shrugged. "I don't know. I've never been sick." They didn't have disease in Upper Synovi, and as Agape struggled to answer, Rayn saw something more important: Nina's apartment.

It wasn't much different from the buildings around it, but he could sense the stories and the giant gun inside, as if the carving on the cement walls called her name out to him. He dashed through the familiar red-brown door into the underhang of the building—

Inside Rayn side-stepped, startled: a screaming fat hunk toppled over the upstairs railing to crash beside him.

On the top landing of the rickety metal stairs above, Nina battled for her life with three Guards.

"Oh no, Nina, hold on, I'm coming!" He stumbled on the stairs. "Wait, wait, wait—"

An enraged yell from Nina, a loud skull-crunching thwack, and a Guard came rolling down almost on top of Rayn.

Rayn pressed himself against the wall out of the way. "Watch it!"

Nina ripped open the door of her apartment, snatched a man inside by the collar, slammed the door on his head, and threw him over the railing, too.

"Uh, wow, Nina—"

The man writhed on his broken back like a turtle, reaching for the small disembodiment pistol on his hip. Nina hoisted her giant blaster over the railing, aimed down, and fired.

Both of the Guards on the first floor disintegrated. Rayn tucked his face into his shirt against the smell of burnt meat and rusted metal, and scrambled up the steps.

Nina turned her anger on him without a second for celebration. Rayn found himself stammering before her heated glare: "I—didn't want to be stuck—"

"You didn't want to be stuck?" she snapped, ripping open her apartment door to show him the mess inside. "You left my door unlocked because you didn't want to be stuck?"

Rayn fumbled. The bed was thrown about the floor, blankets everywhere; muddy, boot-printed food spilled onto the ground from crushed cans.

"I didn't think anything would happen…"

"You're lucky they didn't take my books." She holstered her cannon on her back, and jerked her chin at him. "Your Upworlder wealth destroyed your common sense, and now you're endangering my Neutrality, too. Goodbye, Rayn."

"But why did they even—" The door slammed. Rayn's shoulders drooped. "—want your stuff anyway?"

Rayn stood for a long time atop the landing in front of that door. Alone, outside, locked out again, and again because he failed to lock down his life.

Was that it?

Yes, yes it was, sure, he'd lost his girlfriend. No matter now, and why always compare Nina to *that* girl? Nina! Nina sat breathing on the other side of the door, and had he noticed an abrasion on her wrist? Why? She was Neutral!

Because of…him, maybe?

Rayn clenched his fingers against the rough pants; his breathing slowed into a controlled death-march to which his executioner's heart marked time.

Oh, he was a special kind of mad.

Rayn stalked down the once-magical stairs and out the door, every move slow and measured. His eyes seemed to sharpen focus like the lens of his doorway hall monitor camera back home. His breathing marched, marched, marched…

There wasn't a Guard in sight. Down the street to the left, scattered pamphlets rolled in the grey wind like ancient tumbleweed before mahogany clouds. Down to the right, an unhealthy pale green glow illuminated only piles of trash.

One of the piles of trash twitched and sniffled.

Rayn's march right-faced. His new itchy foot-covers—shoes, per Nina—snuff-snuff-snuffed through dust and broken glass, then stomped to a stop.

"Did you see where the Guards came from?" he asked the pile of old clothes and snot.

The child tucked itself deeper into the pile, face hidden by old plastic and hair covered with dirty cotton.

Rayn folded his hands across his chest. The child had to have seen something.

"Go away," it mumbled.

Rayn blew his breath out through pursed lips, his hand on the back of his neck and fingers raking through his hair. He hadn't seen a person younger than himself in years, so he didn't know how to talk to one. Did they usually have such big heads?

"Does your head…hurt?" Rayn asked.

"What? No!" the child piped with such force the plastic bag fell off his head. Stringy brown and yellow hair laced with sticky threads bounced free under his ears. Rayn saw the dirty tell-tale tracks left behind by old tears on the child's smudged cheeks.

"Are you…okay? Were you crying?"

"No, I'm fine! Thank-you and goodbye!"

Rayn huffed and left, kicking the trash around him. Stupid child. Stupid Prince! Stupid everyone, how dare they!

"Where can I find a Guard?" he roared down the street.

No one answered him, and his common sense began to cool and shape his anger as he went street by street. He would not, of course, charge in and start throwing fists. He would demolish them with logic, with the Prince's promise to honor neutrality.

He recognized the turn of this street, with the shiny black cube building on the corner. Here he'd found the Guards the first time. He would demand to talk to the Prince, and the Prince would sort all of this out.

But then:

"Four cheques, for that business you pulled earlier," snarled a thick, throaty voice behind him.

"Hi Smurl." Rayn drizzled his words in that frigid professionalism he always fed the teachers right before his special complaint got them fired. "I need to talk with the Prince."

He began to turn—

Something cold and hard tickled his spinal cord.

"Don't move," Smurl menaced. "Not a muscle."

In his peripheral vision Rayn saw the other Guards emerge to gather around him, chuckling.

"You want I should get first strike at his face, Smurl?" asked a young pimply-faced teenager.

"After he pays me those four cheques."

"That's not really good incentive," Rayn said. "Don't you see I'd be less inclined to give you money if I know I'm paying for a bruising? Also, I'm Neutral!"

"Like hell you are." The weapon pressed deeper into his spine, and the pimple-teen's eyes lit up in answer to some signal from Smurl. Pimples raised his fist.

Rayn clenched his jaw, eyes narrowed and blazing, too hot and angry for anything but defiance. His nostrils flared.

"You hit him, I hit you, Smurl." Nina's voice! Rayn's chest opened in joyous relief, as if the air itself *longed* to inflate his lungs. He turned his head to see her behind them all, flicking curly auburn hair over her shoulder with a toss of her chin.

Smurl growled.

Nina bared her teeth with a smile.

Smurl raised his hands. "I thought you were Neutral, Nina."

"I am, and so's he," she said. "And around here, I believe Neutrals have protection, and rights to self defense. Or should we report to the Prince the reason four of your number just went missing?"

Someone shoved Rayn towards Nina—he stumbled and whirled, fists raised and head pounding with rage. Smurl kept his hand on his gun and smiled.

"Get, then," he said. "Take your little Upworlder pet back to lick your boots."

Rayn burned.

"Ecosystem, remember," Nina whispered.

"Ecosystem?" he hissed back. "Why did they go after your stuff, then, when you're Neutral?" Her elbow, gentle against his ribs, guided him a few steps across the street as she kept the

Guard station in her cannon's aim.

"Because you left the door unlocked," she said—and loud enough for the Guards to hear: "When you leave out crumbs, it attracts the tiny ants."

Steaming with anger and something like shame, Rayn almost couldn't move beside her, and it took an overwhelming force of logic, and constant glances at the disembodiment cannon, to remind him to take one step after the other until they passed the next corner into a smaller alleyway. They continued in silence. He'd tried. He'd tried to "stand up" for her, and it did nothing! She didn't need him. So how could he make it up to her, and how could she continue to live like this, excusing her oppressors?

"You deserve better," he muttered.

"Oh, I'm aware!"

They pushed through a narrower passageway of bronze bars branching every which way, and the metal twigs made Rayn notice, yet again, that here lived no tree, not a single green thing. Every room in Upper Synovi grew at least one green life form, for oxygen and psychological health, and here without them Rayn imagined himself growing more and more barbaric…

He steeled his will, and took up his stand in front of her, at the head of the alleyway, blocking the exit with arms outspread and fists on each wall.

"You deserve to get out of here, and the Prince owes you," he said. His heart ached worse now, like metal wires and shards tangling against each other, and he had to choke down his next breath. "I can talk to him—I've met him—and if that doesn't work, there's…someone else."

"Who else?"

Rayn looked down. "I don't really want to tell you. I'll make that one a last resort, because I don't think you'd approve."

Her intense gaze seemed to burrow into his forehead. "Why does what I think matter to *you*?" she asked.

He glared back. How could she ask that?

The intensity of his expression made her lift an eyebrow; his face softened, and instead of challenging her he teased, gently, a melancholy smile hinted at the edge of his lips: "You can't tell?"

"Tell what?"

He shrugged and looked away. He couldn't say it outright; he didn't know how much time they had left, if he failed to bring her home. Why ruin what they had before they lost it all?

Then again—

He leaned on his forearm against a cold brick building, running his hand through his hair as he struggled. She hated Agape. She wouldn't want to lose the dignity of making it there on her own.

Still: "Just let me find you a way up."

She smirked at him, butt of her cannon planted on the ground as she leaned on it with hip out to the side. He kept her gaze and refused to swallow, to back down or avert his eyes, even though everything about her made him feel like everything about him required an apology. In the awkward silence, he would have her speak first.

She blinked, but said nothing.

He waited. He'd learned, in his business psychology, in his legal classes, not to speak first. He clung to that memory, to the way his interpersonal power had dominated his past relationships, back in the herd...

And then he gave in, not out of nervousness, but because suddenly it seemed very silly to try to prove his psychological herd manhood to the cannon-wielding alley-woman who lived alone in a concrete box. "I won't ask without your permission," he said. "And maybe you think I'm completely unreliable, after that door thing, but I want to make this happen. I want to take you home. I can't imagine living up there, and never seeing you again. And maybe you don't want to see me, when you get up there. That's fine. But then I want to imagine you happy, not here." He didn't like *asking* things, especially of women, but he muscled through it. Deep breath: "Will you let me try?"

He hated himself for this weakness…

But it was what she needed, for Nina broke her gaze, and looked down where her black boots crushed the red dirt, and smiled. A cool air of happiness blew across Rayn and his heart relaxed.

"You know why I came looking for you?" Nina asked, peering up at him shyly through the corner of her eye.

"Because you're a good person, and you knew I'd get myself killed." It felt deeply odd, and purging, to speak such humiliation, but the ache in his chest seemed somehow good now.

"Absolutely not," she coughed, her smile widening. "I found this."

She drew into her waist satchel, and with a great rustling held out—

The stack of recipes he'd compiled, crunchy and neat in its imperfect ragged bundle.

"I've never met anyone like you," she said. "Look, look at what you made for me!"

Rayn sighed deeply, and stepped forward to take what she held out, and found she didn't let go but instead drew him closer by lowering the stack they both held between them. She stepped in, and laid her gun against the wall as her eyes remained fixed on his face, and she leaned towards him…

A glowing sprite *bulleted* down the alleyway.

It shot between them—Rayn and Nina both stumbled back, almost impaled by the metal forest.

"Hey, watch it!" Rayn yelled, catching his elbow on a rusty spike.  Nina's blaster was now close between them again, cuddled along her muscular arm, and Rayn had never in his life been more frustrated.

"Rayn, this isn't what I brought you here for," Agape scolded. "You're going to get sicker, and she's—you're sharing illness between each other, you!"

"I was just about to—I was just!" Rayn yelled. "If you didn't bring me here to help her get out of this hell-hole, then what is the point of you?"

Rayn *felt* Nina bristle. He turned, and saw the smirk reappear on those bright red lips, shadowing the glisten of her limpid eyes.

"I know you don't like Virtus," Rayn said. "I'm not making excuses, and I know you knew how I got down here."

"I guessed, yes." Her glare did not wane.

Agape wilted, his light flickering as visible smoke puffed off him in almost palpable frustration.  "You're here to save *you*, Rayn."

"I'll go through the operation if you bring her to Upper Synovi." Rayn crossed his arms. "She deserves better."

"She deserves death, according to her disease!" Agape said. "My goal is rarely to get people what they deserve!"

"What do you mean? That's wrong, you can't mean—"

"It's an ecosystem, Rayn," Nina interjected, understanding, apparently, better than he did. "You're still hung up on right and wrong.  I don't believe I'm diseased, but I understand quarantine."

Agape actually turned pink. "No, no, I'm not afraid you'll contaminate anyone, Nina, I'm afraid that Upper Synovi will make your heart *sicker*." He turned to Rayn. "You, you've not even begunyour treatment *down here!*"

"I'll start it when you get her safe passage."

"No, no, you can't *buy* this kind of life like a merchant's snake-oil. We can't cure your heart if your heart's not in the cure!" Agape said.

Rayn threw his hands up in the air. "That's placebo nonsense."

"The placebo effect is a real neurobiological extension of metaphysical faith-based—"

"Stop." Rayn held both palms out to the glow-bug. "Take us to the warehouse. I want to talk to the Prince, and the Invader, and I will do whatever it takes to get Nina a better life."

Agape fell silent, and a soft blue rushed over him before he returned to his pleasant ivory glow. The pale cheeks seemed to turn up into a smile.

"Alright. Follow me, then."

But Nina did not move. She shared a dangerous look with Rayn, her eyes suddenly deadened, and shook her head just a centimeter.

Agape watched for a second, then said: "You can trust. Agape never fails."

"Why do you sometimes refer to yourself in third person?" Rayn asked.

"Because I am Virtu. I am more than the life-form you see before you; I am charity—not pity, or generosity as you would understand it in money and motions, but true charity."

"What?" Nina scowled.

"Because that's just who I am."

Rayn glanced at Nina one more time. She sighed, and charged

and reloaded her gun.

"I think we're all going to regret this."

And so, Rayn followed the glimmering shadow, and behind him, cannon strapped to her back, followed the reluctant Nina, to make a deal with someone else's devil.

# Sight

The warehouse feltdifferent this time, before they even arrived. Rayn's chest didn't change or hurt, and the silence of the twisted orchestra actually unnerved him. The sicker you were, the less you felt, Agape had said…

Nina's footsteps behind him comforted his soul. He had never seen her afraid, and the tension in her jaw, when he looked back, made him want to become strong for her. They crossed the canyons of wooden boxes, Agape's pale light guiding them like a haunted whaler's lamp, and then slipped through the crack in the creaking door.

"Well?" Nina asked.

Dust floated in the dim beams of light from the high windows. Nothing else stirred. Cookie crumbs on one of the boxes towards the back reminded Rayn of the Invader, but otherwise, the palpable plainness almost made him wonder if he hadn't suffered intoxication when he saw this place before.

"Are you sure this is the right…" Rayn squinted. Tall wooden walls squinted back at him through tiny rectangular windows up near the metal paneled roof. It seemed right, but the vast shadows had disappeared, and nowhere did he see ice, or flickering lights, or smoke, or anything but dusty boxes.

"He's—right there in front of you." Agape flickered.

Nina and Rayn both looked at each other, then back across the expanse of the warehouse.

"Where?" she asked.

"Where? What does that mean for a being like him? He flows, he radiates—he does not sit 'here' or stand 'there'—he's everywhere!"

Nina stepped back, smirking, arms crossed. Rayn wondered if Agape had played some kind of trick before; he had never heard the Words with his ears, only in his head, and he had seen some pretty strange things on hallucinogens before…

"Agape, there's nothing here."

Agape tilted his head like a confused poodle, staring into the shadows.

"You know what, I think we're alright, Agape. We'll find the Prince. I'm—" Rayn suddenly saw the bewildered sprite with the same pity he occasionally felt towards Voni. "I hope you're okay."

With that, he grabbed Nina's gloved hand and pulled her out the door. He heard Agape cursing behind him. "This is the third time, sir! Why do you keep doing that? If they don't see you, how can they change heartbeats?"

The one-sided argument faded as Rayn and Nina ducked around the back of the warehouse. Heartbeats again…Rayn wondered how long Voni had spent down here. Despite what he'd said to Agape earlier, about going through any lengths to get Nina to Upper Synovi, he did not want to return home and find himself changed. He turned away from the warehouse not just because he didn't see anything, but because he feared what he might see if he tried too hard.

* * *

Nina and Rayn waited behind the warehouse for a few hours to see if the Prince would show. Rayn wasn't particularly ready to talk directly to the Guards again, but in the back of his mind he'd begun to steel himself for that possibility, too. Nina would know her way back to that station, right?

"Your handwriting is so stiff," Nina smiled, leafing through the pages of recipes. "It's so different. That's what I liked about you at first, just that you were so different from us."

"Stiff doesn't sound good."

"You with your good and bad." She teased with a little elbow to the ribs. But then sighed in a way that made Rayn wonder…

"You wish you had a good and bad," he said.

"Oh, who knows. Be quiet. You wish you had a lady love."

Rayn laughed. "Do I."

"Of course. I was suspicious, at first, with the way you looked at me. So I gave you plenty of opportunities to mess up and get shot. That's how most guys behave if you're kind to them. Like you owe them more."

Rayn furrowed his brow. "Wait, did you invite me in to see if I was worth *shooting*?"

"No, that's too much work. I'm just saying I had my reservations."

"Why did you invite me in, then?"

"I was curious about the Upworld. And you looked completely helpless."

Rayn couldn't hide his cringe. He hated this part of their dynamic. "I want to prove to you that I'm not, but I feel like saying that makes it worse."

"I'd be helpless my first few weeks in your world, too, if I'd never heard of it. They're just ecosystems, Rayn." She waved the recipe stack at him. "You're adaptable. I mean, look at this. Look how unique you are! You learned to write, and immediately wrote a book."

"What else would you do with that ability?" He chuckled. This meant even more to her than he'd intended.

"What a proactive way to think," she sighed, and for the second time her head crept down onto his shoulder.

* * *

The apartment building no longer existed when Rayn and Nina returned for dinner.

In its place, a bonfire spat out sheets of paper and crumbling mortar. Rayn clenched his fingers, seething through his teeth as Nina stood beside him with a face wiped as blank as a freshly swept floor.

"They took absolutely everything." Her voice seemed monotone and empty. "It didn't matter if it was locked or not. They just destroyed it."

"We'll hunt them down," Rayn spat. "The Guards can't get away with all that loot without someone seeing."

On cue, he heard sniffling.

Rayn turned to see the trash-boy down the street, still rubbing his nose in a filthy shirt.

"Where did the Guards go?" Rayn demanded.

This time the boy sunk so far into the trash pile only his wide eyes remained visible. He shook his head over and over. "I don't know. I don't know."

"Yes you do." He tried to soften his tone. "I promise they won't find out if you tell me."

"What can *you* do?" the boy sneered.

"Where did they go?" The words squeezed through clenched

teeth. "Look, I'm guessing you know what it's like to lose everything. So does she." He pointed. "Help me out here!"

"They didn't go down that road to the docks." Meaning, of course, the opposite. The boy retreated back under the blanket and did not speak again.

"That's back towards the warehouse we came from," Nina said. "We must have just missed them on the side street."

"The Prince will be there this time for sure," Rayn said, whirling to leave.

Nina shook her head. "Why are you doing this? This isn't your business. This is picking a fight with the lion."

"The lion owes you."

"No, I asked why are *you* doing this?"

Rayn turned back towards her. In his rush he'd forgotten the distance between them that constantly tugged at his mind, and now with her question it yawned, obvious, and huge. The gun on her back, the home he'd return to...

He didn't want to start anything. They might never see each other again.

He couldn't help it. They might never see each other again.

He held out his hand.

She gave him hers. He snapped her close with a tug, and lifted her over the nearest pile of parts and plastic, not because she needed his help, but because she deserved the honor of a queen. They paused then, hand in hand, his arm draped almost around her waist, hips nearly touching. Her eyes waited and watched as her lips fluttered; he could feel the heat radiating from her core.

"You know why," he said, scanning her eyes. Did she understand? He didn't have time to find out. They had to find the Prince. He released her, his breathing ragged, and it felt like ripping a bandage off a scab: he wanted her close.

But he held himself responsible for her losses, and he held himself responsible for paying her back. He sprinted the last few streets towards the warehouse.

* * *

Back in front of the warehouse, about thirty Guards lounged on the barrels and crates around the front, laughing. Rayn and Nina watched them from behind the boxes; Rayn twitched his head towards another path in the maze of packing junk, and Nina nodded.

They almost reached the door.

"Figured you'd come looking for us, after that," Smurl chuckled from behind.

How could someone that fat stay so stealthy?

Rayn whirled, fist flying. Smurl grabbed his arm and twisted, reversing the force of the blow. Rayn cried out in pain.

"I'll make sure you never find the Prince. I'll make sure you never go back!" Smurl snarled, pinning Rayn to the ground on his back with a heavy knee in his chest.

Nina was screaming. Nina! Rayn thrashed like a skewered fish. He rolled on top of Smurl, smashing the man in the face with both fists balled into one punch. He jumped up, stomped down—both feet jammed into Smurl's ample stomach.

Smurl grabbed Rayn's ankles, rolled over, and smashed the Upworlder to the ground. Rayn's body shuddered, unprepared for the hard cement after training on spongy floors.

"Agh!" Rayn clenched his teeth, scrambled backwards, and kicked Smurl in the face. "Why'd you do that to her place, man?" Rayn shouted.

"Oh, she'll get repaid," Smurl smirked. "She'll get repaid in *man*."

"Get off me!" Nina roared.

Rayn growled and ran. He dashed up the side of a crate, leapt off it as Smurl charged, and kicked the neighboring stack of boxes into the burly man's face.

Nina's glove grabbed his wrist and yanked him through the warehouse door.

Rayn slammed and bolted it behind them.

"That's not going to hold them," Nina panted, eyes wide. "They—they have my blaster. I don't fight well without it. I was caught by surprise or we could've annihilated them all. Now there will be more."

"They're your ecosystem's sharks. Idiots attracted to blood," Rayn scowled.

"Very poetic," Nina shuddered. She rubbed her wrists, as if to scrub off the memory of the Guard's hands. Her hair fell all across her face—Rayn reached to brush it aside—

He paused, his chest constricting. "May I?" he whispered.

"I love that question," she laughed through her breathlessness. "You're so different. You...you ask permission, with every movement. I love the question!"

His hand hovered by her temple. "You may love the question, but you didn't answer it," he chuckled back.

"Oh—fine, whatever." Her pale face made her dark eyes look wider, and her lips tightened as she wrapped her arms around herself. Rayn pushed her hair behind her ear, biting his lip. She was like a unicorn de-horned, or a de-clawed lion, and he did not relish her sudden weakness. He felt that somehow he had caged a hurricane. At her most vulnerable he most wanted to keep distance, keep her dignity. But he also most wanted—

"I'm sorry," he whispered. "I—really want to hold you right now."

A strange choking sound escaped her throat. She hurled herself into him, her fingers clawing his biceps. He felt her heart beating against his chest like salmon thrashing in a net.

"Hold me," she whispered.

* * *

Rayn could not hold her long. The din outside grew to a roar; he heard laughter, but no one touched the door. The Guards knew as well as Rayn and Nina did that without Nina's blaster the warehouse was just a holding cage. His heart pounded against hers, his blood equal parts rage for her and fear for himself. *I can't believe you're fighting me over a woman,* Wyn had said. *Just a woman.*

There was no such thing.

"A stranger. You're that lovely stranger everyone meets, just for the briefest time, and then never wants to let go," he muttered into her hair.

A glimmer caught his eye. Screams rang out, not outside, but in his head.

Agape.

"I think there's a back way out of here," Rayn said. He ran to the far corner of the warehouse, following the dim phantom light. It ebbed and flowed from under a crack in a crate.

"Help me," he grunted, straining against the crate. Nina shouldered up beside him, and the crate slid free to reveal a rotten wooden door in the back wall.

Rayn shoved through it, and stumbled into the neighboring warehouse.

He froze.

Behind him, he heard shuffling as Nina entered after him, and scraping as she covered the door with another crate, but that seemed eons and miles away. His eyes remained glued to the rafters…

"He bleeds," Nina murmured in surprise, stepping back with repulsion.

Agape's torso lay on the floor, bright red liquid draining from a gash in his stomach and a hole in his neck.

Rayn did not reply. The ceiling terrified him. Little by little it came into focus.

"What's wrong with you?" Nina elbowed him.

Gore not meant for human eyes dripped above him. As he stared, another world grew into focus; Agape's body solidified, and Nina and the warehouse became ethereal like a mist.

"Welcome to True Synovi, Rayn," said the Prince, twice the size of any man, crouched on hawk-feet on the rafter as he held up Agape's dripping head. "I heard you were looking for me."

Rayn stared at the little light being. It seemed to twitch, as if still partially alive, and a vivid memory of its gentle air filling his lungs in space suddenly flooded his chest.

"W—why?"

"What's wrong?" Nina's elbow on his ribs felt like a mist, or perhaps a memory of an elbow far away.

The Prince tossed the glowing head over his shoulder. "It's shocking, I know, Rayn. But I'm saving you from slavery." He licked his fingers.

The Prince shook off his hood as if shaking off shackles, revealing a face that to Rayn looked like a three-dimensional mirror, only with long, flowing black hair, and a few scattered scars. He casually jumped from the rafter to land near Rayn.

This time, as the shadow fell over him and Nina, the silence in Rayn's heart really felt like death. There was no ache, but also no relief—only numbness.

"Agape never…did anything…wrong," Rayn said.

"Proselytizing is illegal, Rayn. Not just down here, but up there, too. You know that."

"But he wasn't forcing himself on anyone, just talking…"

"Rayn, who are you talking to?" Nina asked.

Rayn stared at her, and understood, and hoped she would understand, too, instead of thinking him crazy. "Nina, I can see the Prince," he said. "I'm not sure why neither of us could see anything earlier, or why you can only see Agape, but he just killed—the Prince did that." Rayn pointed at the body on the floor.

"To save you," the Prince interjected. "These things enslave your mind. You'd find yourself emptied, insane, pouring your soul into those who don't deserve it and throwing yourself over and over into an empty abyss of problems that don't exist. People don't need to be saved, they just need a leg up every now and then. You have to look out for yourself, Rayn. I am."

Rayn wanted to hear the counterpoint, not because he doubted the Prince's logic, but because he couldn't forget the little sprite's passion, the earnest honesty of its pain when he argued with it; the worshipful kiss it gave that girl who'd turned into a star.

As he wanted, he saw the Invader in the shadows, far in the back of the room, cradling the discarded head.

The Prince followed his gaze and scowled. "Excuse me, but who are you here for, him or me?" the Prince asked.

"Whoever can help my friend, I guess," Rayn said.

"Oh, that would be me," the Prince said, clapping his hands.

Something like a chariot appeared beside him, gilded over black engravings in intricate arabesques. "Passage for both of you, back to Upper Synovi. It's equipped with oxygen and pressurized; you just have to press this. There's a map, too. Steering's here."

Rayn reached to touch it, and glanced at Nina. She saw it, too, and looked back at him. "A spaceship?" she asked.

"Yeah," Rayn said. "The Prince says…" He fingered the smooth, rounded warps and shapes in the beautiful surface. "To take you to Upper Synovi," he half-finished.

Nina didn't touch. She looked around the room, and crossed her arms. "I don't like that you speak to beings I can't see, Rayn, and I don't like random objects appearing out of nowhere."

"I know, I don't…I don't either." Rayn muttered.

"What are you waiting for?" the Prince asked. "Don't you love her?"

Rayn looked over at the Invader. The Invader didn't look up from cradling the head.

"I would do anything to get her a better life," Rayn said.

What if he really was sick, though? And what if she really needed a cure, too? He feared meeting her in Upper Synovi, a husk of her former self, and regretting this moment. He hadn't *been* a real person up there, and he wouldn't wish that on anyone; and more than anyone, on her.

"How much time do I have to decide?" he asked. Then, realizing suddenly how that sounded, deciding for someone else right in front of her: "What do you want to do?" he asked her.

"I think I don't want anything to do with any of these things. Not the spaceship, not the Prince, not the Invader, no one," she said. "I want to find another way."

"That could take years, though," Rayn said. "And you have no more money."

"You asked what I want, and that's my answer." She raised both hands palm out.

"Okay, but then—how do *I* get home? I don't have a job here, and I can't just mooch off of you until you find a way up," Rayn said. "You said it yourself, I'm useless here."

"I don't know, Rayn. Maybe you take this way, and I'll meet you later."

The suggestion hurt. Why would she say that, after what they'd been through? He didn't want to spend any time away from her; her practicality seemed so cold and cruel!

He didn't understand that practicality is often a disguise for fear.

"If you push for it, I'll go," Nina sighed finally. "If you're really certain this is the way."

"That's not fair," Rayn said. "I don't want to force you into something knowing you hate it! Then it's my fault if it fails!" He looked back towards the Invader. Why didn't the Being say something? Back to Nina: "Maybe we just need more time to think about it."

The Prince huffed like a horse, shrinking to human size to cross his arms like a teenager. "You may think eternal beings like myself have a lot of time to waste on favors for nobodies, but I do not."

"Forgive me, sir," Rayn stammered at the red ooze still glowing on the Prince's fingertips. "I—I think I want a second opinion. Is that okay? Can I decide in a few minutes?"

"A second opinion?" The Prince bloomed to several times his height, pixelated again. "A second opinion?"

Rayn choked. "I'm not trying to offend you. Again, I'm very

Neutral. I want to hear from all sides, and I'm—yes."

He coughed, and ran for the shadows.

"I don't want you talking to that thing," the Prince hissed, sliding in front of him. "He'll poison your mind."

"I know you're trying to protect me, sir, and I appreciate that very much," Rayn said, smelling saccharine syrup on the Prince's breath. They were much closer to the Being now, and he could see it still staring at the little head, its solid ice face silent and unreadable. "I'm not deciding to join him or anything. I just want to be…thorough?"

"Decide on your own, like a man. You don't need to ask for any opinion but your own." The Prince folded his arms.

"Why do you care?" Rayn asked. "You don't have anything to hide. Why is it so difficult to get to this guy? First he's cooped up, then invisible, then you're killing his guys—and I get that he kills your guys, too, but—this just feels weird."

The Prince sighed. "'The fruit of your lips, like wine.' 'I desire your Words more than honey, than much fine gold,'" he quoted. "You don't understand. A few seconds with him can destroy your mind forever. Don't you see? He's radioactive, addictive! You felt what he did to your blood-organ."

"My blood organ?" Rayn snickered. "You mean my heart?"

"Yes, sure, that gross thing." The Prince waved his giant hand. "For your own good, you must decide on your own. I want to elevate you to stand on your own, without crippling dependence."

Rayn looked over the Prince's shoulder, to the ice-giant now towering over them in the much nearer shadow. "Why don't you say anything?" he shouted.

"I said, don't!" The Prince hissed, as if his enemy couldn't hear if he whispered. "Don't, or I will have to end you!"

"*End* me? Hey, you, Invader, why aren't you doing anything? Don't you care that he killed your friend?" Rayn shouted.

"That's it." The Prince snatched Rayn's throat, and suddenly Rayn didn't feel very neutral. "This is for your own good, little mind."

Suddenly the Prince was gripping Rayn's skull like a husband opening a lid, twisting off the Upper Synovian's head. Rayn's neck screamed on the left; the pressure from the fingers on his scalp threw him into wild thrashing. Nina darted forward—another hand from the Prince threw her back against the wall with skull-cracking thwack—

"Invader, help," Rayn croaked.

"Finally," boomed the Words.

With a swat the Prince went flying, taking Rayn with him. A giant hand caught the Prince's head like a baseball in a mitt before they hit the wall. "Let go," the Words blasted, shaking the Prince by the head like a child might thrash a doll.

"You let go!" The Prince shrieked. Rayn could breathe now through the loosening grip, and began to kick. Still, tentacles shot out from the cloak to embrace him; still, claws dug into his scalp.

"Let me run my own world! Mind your own business!" The Prince screamed.

"You hate them anyway. Why do you want them?" The Invader's wrist flicked again, and the whole world seemed to shake. Rayn couldn't imagine how the Prince could hold on, with the gale force blowing at them that almost seemed to rip off Rayn's skin.

"You can't manage an ecosystem! You screw with natural selection, you honor fleshbags while your sprites serve like slaves—"

The Prince's own ranting distracted him, and with one more universe-ending shake, Rayn tumbled free onto the dusty floor, rolling over to the wall and almost bumping into Nina.

The Invader gave the Prince's skull one more vicious squeeze with an enraged growl, then dropped him like a microphone.

The Prince coughed, breathing hard at the Invader's feet. Rayn was breathless himself, and here, so close to the visible, glowing edge of the Invader's now flaming energy field, his chest seemed to fill with tumbling metal spikes. The complex *detail* of what he now saw pulsed his head with such pressure he thought his eyeballs would explode.

The agony made him wheeze.

The Prince saw this, and smirked. "You only help them when you feel like it," he grunted. "They suffer so much because you won't just tell them plainly what's going on."

The Invader knelt; the Prince cringed, but the Invader did not strike. "Had you a child," his Words rolled in a soft grumble. "You would know what it is like to play music with her sitting on your lap. She bangs out one note over and over, but your hands, around her, create the music. I would never deny her the joy of her one little note, the one thing she can choose, by letting her know the music isn't hers."

"Screw off," the Prince spat. "You can pretend you're like them, like you know what it is to breed and to eat and to play the stupid piano with stupid flesh fingers, but you're not like them. You're like me. Yin to my Yang!"

"We are not Yin and Yang," the Invader said. "Dark and light coexist, but nothingness and somethingness cannot. I alone contain the Yin and the Yang, without you; I contain the balance between spaces, the best of dark and light. You! You are the void, the grey, the neither and the none, and as nature abhors a vacuum so I abhor you."

The Prince hacked and shuddered, shivering in the nearness of the heat or the cold—Rayn could not tell which, because it seemed like snowflakes on fire fell from the stone Invader's grassy hair.

"I will make them hate you," the Prince laughed through clenched teeth as tears rolled down his cheeks. He seemed to be in such intense pain. Rayn felt it, too, the searing closeness, and backed against the wall. He reached for Nina; she cradled her hurt head and swatted him away.

"Let me heal you," the Invader whispered to the Prince.

"Freedom over tyranny!"

"Then freely die of your disease, but keep it to yourself." The Invader pinned the Prince with one hand.  Pixelated liquid splashed around his fingers—the other hand dove through the shapes, and peeled back the cloak. "Look, Rayn."

The open, skeletal chest held machinery, wires and gears, engulfed in tumorous red pulsing growth. With each beat, Rayn felt his own heart leap, and each time his chest rolled in that painful sharp rhythm, the tumor slurped and vibrated as if electrocuted by an invisible force.

Rayn drew his arms across his chest like a woman protecting bare breasts from the cold, and the Invader dropped the cloak.

"Fine," the Prince sputtered. "That's just fine." The Prince dissolved through the floor with the hiss of a candlewick crushed between wet fingers.

And Rayn looked around at a world now ruined.

# True Synovi

Rayn swore, over and over, slamming his fist against the dusty floor.

"What on earth is wrong with you," Nina groaned, cupping the back of her head with both hands. "You're alive after whatever that was. Shut up."

Rayn didn't have time to ask what she'd been able to see. He'd seen what he needed to destroy his life. It wasn't just the reveal of the heart machine. It was the way the Invader's intricate solid form seemed now like the best tree, the best wind, the best stone and fire and the best manta ray, the best of all natural beauty at the same time, as if his genetics contained the source code for existence; the fact that the Invader didn't touch him to free him, but gripped the Prince and shook, keeping the edge of his own deadly force field away from Rayn's implodable flesh; and the way Agape's broken form now dissolved into the Invader's gentle fingertips with the literal scent of a smile—

"The Prince was right about the wine," Rayn coughed to the Invader. "I'll never be able to escape you now. How did this happen? How did the Prince get the pitch of my heart?"

"He inserted a genetic mutation into your species' introns eons ago, and along the way adapted his heart to match your own," The Invader said. "But I've created a way to reset your code. It was a difficult solution: in my presence is healing, and fullness of joy, but you cannot access my presence because my radioactive glory, my forcefield, counter-reacts your broken pitch, and destroys you."

"So…what's the answer?" Rayn asked.

"I found the answer through pain. The Prince does not understand, but pain serves a deeper biological purpose than survival. It is the impetus of evolution—the thing that makes us greater than we are. My pain shields you from my own glory; my pain is the lead plate shielding you from the nuclear reaction between my field and your heart. Even now—for my glory is enormous, and without this shield, would touch the entire world at once. But like that lead plate, my pain captures the imbalance, the damage, the released radioactivity of your brokenness, into my perfect balance. My pain changes us both. Or, put another way, when I am close to the Prince's heart, I let him hurt me, and re-channel the wicked energy of his machine into healing for you. The metaphysics is complicated, and he thinks me a sick fool, but through this solution, I can reset you, and bring you near to me. *That* is the reason I put up with all this." The Invader gestured, and his wave seemed to encompass not just the moments of his personal torture, but all the wrong in all of history. "Because through my pain, you can be healed. Won't you let me reset you, Rayn?"

Another pang pierced Rayn's chest; he shook his head, trying to gain clarity through the discomfort: "If he's feeding off my heart while I'm alive, what happens when I die?"

"Your consciousness is subsumed into his machine signal."

"What's that like?"

"You will be trapped in the Prince's own inner torment."

Ugh. "What about when he dies?"

"He will not," said the Invader. "He is eternal. To kill him, I will imprison him outside of existence, in his own torment, with those he ate."

"That's so confusing," Rayn groaned.

Something gripped his shoulder. "Rayn," Nina said, grabbing the wall to pull herself up. Rayn's eyes met hers, and as he did she began to solidify and the Invader faded.

Rayn could punch himself for not checking her head. "Oh gosh, Nina, are you okay?"

"I've had a concussion before, I don't need your pity," she snapped. "But you! You need to continue your hallucination later!" She jerked her head towards the wall. "I can hear them in the neighboring warehouse!"

"Actually, we're here."

The front door blew in behind them. Rayn and Nina stumbled back, but before they could get anywhere Regiment IV poured in around them, disembodiment blasters humming.

"The Prince told me I might find you here," grinned the curly black-haired man Rayn remembered as Kohn, from Agape's fight in the alleyway. Behind him stood Smurl, and the gray man from the public execution.

Nina grabbed Rayn, and shoved him behind her, raising her fists to defend him. Smurl's hands convulsed, and he rushed at Nina with his tongue dangling—

But Kohn threw an arm straight out into Smurl's path; the fat suck grunted as he hit the clothesline. Black locks bounced as Kohnpursed his lips and shook his head.

"Nina, is it?"

"I'm Neutral, Kohn," she hissed. "Your freak Smurl burned down my home. I've always opposed the Traitors. You have my records."

"We will reimburse you. And transport you to the top of Upper Synovi. The Prince has commanded it," Kohn bowed.

"I don't want the Prince's weird convoluted space-chariot. I want normal transportation that normal people take. With one of you in it so I know it won't explode."

Kohn bowed. "As you request."

"I want that degenerate to leave the room, right now," Nina pointed to the gray man. Kohn nodded, and the man left.

"And I want him punished," Nina pointed to Smurl.

"I will take your views into consideration. I apologize for the misunderstanding."

So reasonable. No devil's price, no signature in blood. Rayn's head pounded; he looked around for the Invader, and this time saw no one but Guards, boxes, and dust.

"Looking around for a rescue, Rayn?" Kohn smiled.

"No, I'm—Neutral…"

"You know the Invader won't interfere if you're surrounded. It's something we've discovered about his nature, you see; too many of us would die if he reached past us for you, what with his radioactive energy field, and our healthy human hearts." He flipped a lock of hair behind his shoulder. "He loves his enemies, you see."

Rayn's head pounded. Kohn stepped towards him, around Nina.

"But you cannot love your enemies without hating your friends." Kohn leaned in; Rayn could smell acid on his breath. "That's what makes a Traitor, isn't it?"

Nina slid between them again; Kohn stepped back and laughed. "And who wants a traitor as a friend?"

"He's no Traitor. I'll vouch for him," Nina said. "He's been a bit confused since he arrived, and he can see the Prince, but he's Neutral."

Kohn stiffened. "How do you know he can see the Prince?"

"There was a big kerfuffle in here just now." Even now, Rayn loved her diction, the over-read intellectualism that just did not fit the edgy image of the leather-clad blaster-wielder. "A misunderstanding."

"I see. Well, I'm sure we can work past that. Rayn? Is there something you still need to understand? Or are you satisfied to join Nina in the comforts…" Kohn waved his arm grandly, as if transforming the very warehouse to that symbiotic world of Above. "…Of Upper Synovi?"

Nina's eyes widened at the gesture, and a relieved laugh escaped her. "It just hit me," she glowed. "Rayn, this is our chance!"

A fierce triumph blazed in her eyes, filling him with joyous ache again. He wanted to say it, to guarantee a future where he could meet her in the hallway, wrap her in his arms, and laugh about books. His whole body warmed at the thought…"I think I love you," he murmured.

"What?" she leaned in to hear.

Kohn's acid-breath big jaw mouth interrupted. "Hello, do we need further discussion or not?"

Rayn's fingers pushed through his hair, as if he could erase the wrinkling of his brow by scrubbing. He remembered her heart beating against his, and still gazing at her face, spoke to Kohn. "Tell her about the heartbeats."

"What?" Kohn's laugh spat out like a snort from his lips.

Rayn turned, shoulders square. "Tell her about the heartbeats."

Kohn raised his eyebrows. "Why can't you tell her? Would it sound less far-fetched, from a man with authority?"

Rayn reeled under the insult. He glared at the floor. "I saw the Prince's heart," he muttered.

"I know," said Kohn. "And he spoke well of you. But your interest in his private health matters makes me curious about your allegiance." Kohn's bright blue eyes sparkled when he said this, daring, just daring Rayn to pry down this path. Rayn knew Kohn could have just laughed him off—but Kohn wanted Rayn to know he *knew*.

"Why are you making this difficult?" Rayn wondered.

"Because the Prince is as much my weapon, our weapon, as he is his own being. We'll kill the Invader. We'll be free to control the world's destiny. The pitches of our hearts do not damn us—they're who we are. We are born this way."

Rayn moaned. These kinds of conversations wearied him into Neutrality in the first place. "I just want to go back." Back to the way things were.

"We can transport you back. Simply promise never to return."

Rayn opened his mouth to say yes—

He longed. He saw a future in Upper Synovi wondering every day what would have happened if he'd said no. He saw an organic architectural structure deciding his life, leaving him only choices between levels of comfort, never any real decisions or reasons to strive.

And beyond that, the giant Being, whose flaming eyes awoke a drunken hunger Rayn did not know he could feel—

Speaking of hunger, he *still* had not eaten.

"You know what, I'm just really really needing food right now," Rayn chuckled nervously, trying to break out some casual spirit. "Maybe we can pick this up another day."

"Another day? Rayn, this is my chance!" Nina said.

"Yes, Rayn. Let's get you out of here, and never come back,"

Kohn smiled.

Rayn clenched his fists and almost squealed in frustrated anxiety. "Alright, yes! Sure, let's do that." He would just ask Agape to bring him back or something. Or maybe Voni knew how to get to the lowest levels, and then he could ask about the heart thing there. He didn't want to live the rest of his life wondering about this ache!

Ask Voni? A part of him almost vomited.

"But, like, you know, if I did want to visit here..." Rayn's small voice said to the floor.

"What was that, Rayn? I couldn't hear," Kohn mocked. Rayn looked him in the eye and knew the leader had heard just fine. Rayn envisioned the girl beaten on the platform and lost all nerve.

"I'm ready to go home," he said.

"Good. Now as proof of your good will...I smell the sprite Agape on you. Where is he?"

Rayn stammered. "He's dead, the Prince—"

"No, you have the scent. You've been with the Invader. Agape is regenerating, right now, somewhere around you. Where?"

"I don't know, but I can ask." The innocence of his statement masked a sudden, desperate hope. Yes, yes, he would settle this and decide, and not die. "I'll be right back!"

He pointed an awkward little smiling pair of "finger guns," and tried to push through the herd of Guards; they looked at Kohn with their weapons raised.

Kohn raised an eyebrow and nodded for them to move.

"Rayn..." Nina said.

Rayn ran. He shook his head, and tried to focus, but could not see the Invader anymore, not even in the deepest shadows here in the back of the warehouse. He found himself muttering to the back wall.

"Look, I know you're still here. May I just—ask one more question?"

The Words answered as if inserted into Rayn's head again; he saw nothing. "Yes."

"Can't we just get rid of the machine?" Rayn asked. "Why does there have to be a choice between anyone? Just destroy the machine, and everyone will be free, right?"

"Rayn," said the Words. "What happens when two waves meet, exactly opposite?"

Rayn had taken physics. "They cancel each other out, right?"

"Yes. So if your pitch and his are the same, the reverberating wave from his destroyed heart will cancel out all heart-waves tuned to his, destroying them and killing you all. Of course we must turn off the feeder eventually. But first I will save as many of you as I can."

"So we're all feeding him, no matter what."

"Yes."

"Unless we get the operation, he wins. No matter how nice we are or whatever."

"Yes."

"So no one's Neutral, then."

"Rayn, you don't have much time. I'm not going to sell this to you. If I adjust the pitch of your heart, it will be a full-blown genetic and spiritual alteration. It will hurt. Your whole life will be different. But your life will be saved, and it will be a worthwhile life."

Agh, no. No, Rayn did not want to decide anything right now; he would talk his way home and then suck up his pride and ask Voni what he knew. He jogged back to the throng, and they re-gathered around him.

He really wished they wouldn't.

"Well?" Kohn asked. "Where is Agape?"

And just then, by awful misfortune, or perhaps a nasty trick of the Invader's, Rayn saw the sprite glimmering outside the open door behind the Guards, drinking sunlight and shivering as its body flowed into its head and it regenerated.

Rayn quickly looked away, at Nina's face, but there he seemed to see the sprite in the reflection in her eyes.

It was fine. The Virtu could handle itself in a fight, right?

Well…like that, though…

"So, not any of my business, but, ah, what do you want with the Virtu?" Rayn asked Kohn, still looking at Nina.

Kohn's grin widened, revealing more teeth and stretching his cheeks.

"Um," Rayn swallowed. "I still don't know where he is. I couldn't get the Invader to appear and talk and all—"

A fist in the face. Rayn's nose bridge exploded. His left eye flashed blinding lights.

Nina exclaimed something; "I like the truth," Kohn laughed, and shrugged.

"Yeah, you genuinely enjoy your job, don't you?" Rayn blurted, hand over his injured eye.

Kohn licked thin lips. "Where is the Virtu?"

Rayn stared at the giant of a man as his eye blasted pain-signals through his head. Even if it *could* regenerate, Rayn couldn't wish a second death on anyone. He just couldn't. "I don't—"

"Rayn, if you know, say so!" Nina hissed.

"I'm sorry, I—"

"Rayn!"

"Bring me the disintegration powder," said Kohn.

Nina cried out and threw herself at Kohn, gripping his arm. "No, no, please let me—let me talk to him. I'll find out, and I'll tell you where the Virtu is. Please, just calm down!"

She seemed to need calming herself. Kohn raised an eyebrow and his left nostril widened, thoroughly amused. "Very well. You have a moment."

The Guards withdrew; Nina snatched Rayn's wrist and yanked him across the warehouse floor. He stumbled after her. "I don't know what to do, Nina, I don't want to put you in danger either—"

"Will you shut up?!" she snapped, whirling to grip his shoulders. He saw her eyes, and for once he could read her face. She stammered something as her cheeks flushed, her lips trembled, and her shoulders heaved. The emotional storm took her in waves; Rayn stared bewildered into her ocean.

Tears streamed down her face.

Rayn choked. He wanted to shake her, drag her back into happiness, do anything to make her stop. "Why the heck are you crying?" He broke out the cold practicality she'd shared earlier. "You barely know me!"

"Because I've never met anyone like you!" She shook him. "I've never wanted to spend so much time with anyone! You make me feel gentle, and warmer—you make me want to care for someone. You listen to me and learn from me, and care whether or not I want you. No one's like you, a whole new world to me, in yourself, and I—" She punched his chest. It didn't hurt, but he cringed. "I don't know what's wrong with you now! What happened back there, with the screaming and the flying around in the air? What are you doing?"

Rayn covered his eyes with one hand and allowed himself a hollow laugh. "It figures you'd tell me how you feel *now*. Just my luck. I can't even kiss you; I'll bleed all over you."

She laughed through her tears and grabbed his face in her hands. "I'm so lost right now," she cried. Her warm, wet palms pressed his cheeks as her fingers trembled. He felt her finger stick in his blood.

"I'm lost, too."

"What happened?" she whispered.

He searched her eyes, and saw only pain. He closed his, and told her.

He told her everything he knew, everything both sides had told him since he'd first arrived, and about the battles he'd seen, about the cookies and the star-goddess and the ice-then-grass-then-stone Invader, and about the hearts.

"It's all propaganda, Rayn," Nina whispered.

Rayn cringed, and held his injured eye. "I know, Nina, but I—I saw that girl, from the execution—she turned into something incredible. I can't describe it, but I'm haunted by it. I want to know—if his *friends* become like that, what is he like? He fought like a terror, but the way he healed the girl, like—"

Rayn caught himself. Nina was staring at him like he'd eaten his best friend alive.

He lowered his voice. "I'm not saying I want it, just—if the Invader changed my heartbeat, it would be—interesting to find out what that's like."

"No!" Her hands became fists. She stepped back, just holding them still in the air, trembling. Her teeth ground. "No! The sprites can't steal you away, too, they can't!" She collapsed to the ground on her knees, fists over her face, sobbing. He knelt by her. His nose still dripped blood, and though he wanted to wrap his arm around her shaking shoulders, he did not touch her. He felt as awkward and cold as if he'd found her dead. "You were too good to be true," she cried. "They had to take you. I always lose in the end."

"Nina, you're all about how things aren't all or nothing…" His hand crept to her shoulder-blade. "You could try it too—I'm sure they'll change it back, if you don't like it, or at least let me try it for you and then you'll know—"

"I will not sacrifice my heart to an experiment, and I will not lose the spot in Upper Synovi that I've worked for all my life!" She snarled and knocked his hand away. She slashed her sleeve over her face, as if clawing or smashing the tears dry, and scrambled to her feet.

"I can't hurt the Virtu just because I'm afraid, though! Hell, I may be a useless coward, but I'm not a jerk!"

"It's just a wisp of wind! It's not even a person like us!" She gestured, as if to say more, but the tears came back. She wiped her face again. She struggled—and finally she ran to the other side of the warehouse, her boots slapping cement.

She looked small over there by all those Guards. Rayn saw Kohn say something to her; she turned away without a word.

Kohn smiled, looking away from Nina to sneer into Rayn's eyes.

Rayn's shoulders slumped. "Well, I'm dead," he muttered to the wall behind him. "So change my heartbeat, then. Just to rob the Prince of the last few minutes of food from me. And screw you if you're actually just like him," Rayn finished.

Nothing felt different, and he heard no reply.

His stomach gurgled, and he cursed. "Dang am I hungry."

The Guards waited for him, filling both the far doorway and the secret side-door with their bodies.

Rayn rose to his feet. His muscles tensed, and right now he wanted with all of his being only to cling to the wall, throw away his dignity, and beg as pitifully as he could to stave off the punishment.

He forced his legs to step forward.

Even as he walked, his mind threw frantic escape scenarios at him. He just needed someone to throw two Guards away from the door long enough for Agape to fly him out…

Rayn stood before Kohn, arms relaxed at his sides, chin tilted up so he could see into the giant chiseled face.

"Well?" asked Kohn.

"Agape is two blocks down the street in a little house—"

"Liar."

Thick fingers gripped his biceps as two Guards threw their weight against him. Rayn's back slammed against cement. They pinned him; they yanked open his shirt, their breath hot against his face and chest.

Kohn opened a little package of white powder.

Rayn heard Nina suck in a gasp as Kohn stood far above him and tilted. Grains floated down onto his left shoulder, scattering across his chest—

His skin faded in the dim light, flesh replaced by agony. He did not break or peel; no blood flowed from the tiny wounds. Specks of arm, and chest just—disappeared—where the grains touched.

Rayn couldn't tell if the scream belonged to him or Nina. The white powder gnawed through skin, muscle, bone and out to the other side, burning, and Rayn saw himself disappearing, and his head rang, overwhelmed with the sensation overflow, and the rest of his body seized, and his arm continued to scream; *scream!* Kohn's face beamed, eyes closed over parted, panting lips. Somewhere in the distance Rayn heard the man "Mmmm…" Rayn wanted to vomit.

At last, the powder dissolved through him and reached the floor.

Rayn panted, eyes closed as sweat and something else wet beaded on his cheeks. He could feel light and air streaming through tiny holes in his shoulder and chest, and the pain dimmed from a sharp burn to a low, aching throb.

"I enjoyed that," said Kohn.

"I could tell," Rayn groaned.

"And Agape?"

Rayn opened his eyes to glare. "You can tell the Prince you're the reason I'm joining the Invader."

Kohn's smile finally melted.

The man pounced on top of Rayn, snarling. His knee shoved into Rayn's abdomen, but the Upworlder didn't have time to register the blunt pain before the entire package of powder spilled across his face and chest. He couldn't see. A calloused hand rubbed rough grains across his skin, his eyes. The burn became a sharp smell, an acrid taste as someone forced it into his mouth, and his whole body thrashed. He could feel—he could only feel—

He could no longer hear himself scream.

# Goodbye

Nina tried to hold herself back. She could not lose Upper Synovi now, she could not! She ground her teeth together and pinched herself.

But she could not stop the terror rising in her veins.

She hurled herself at the Guard in front of the door, her whole body one clenched fist to his midriff. He fell like a domino, knocking down the man beside him. She ripped his disembodiment blaster from his back; she fired into the crowd before her. Men disappeared as she flailed.

As they drew their weapons, the Virtu shot out of nowhere. Its glow had faded to a dim aura, but in the confusion it had enough strength to snatch Rayn. Nina felt it breeze past her as it dragged Rayn through the gap she'd made—cool liquid flowed over her hand—

She found herself dangling by the wrist in the air.

Below them, Guards tumbled out the warehouse door.

"The gun is too heavy!" cried the Virtu. "Agape cannot carry your weapon today!"

She dropped it, and clung with both hands to the strand-like arm holding her wrist. They doubled over the warehouse roof. Guards raced into the streets, trying to distance themselves from the warehouse so they could fire over it.

Nina's fallen gun shattered among them, blue light zapping and bouncing across the men. Its explosion took out at least six.

"Put your face in my hand!" Agape ordered. "We go into space, now!"

Nina did a pull-up and buried her face in its shoulder. They broke into the brown clouds, water and dirt freezing around them for just an instant…

And then they floated in a vastness Nina had never imagined. Pinpoints of light she recognized as Stars, from her books, glittered around her like the memory of her mother's dress. Agape began to melt down into an amoebic, unrecognizable shape; it flowed around Nina and Rayn as a fragrant, palpable perfume.

"I cannot move anymore," it said. "I am broken and weary. The pain in your heart, and his heart, I feel in my whole body. I must rest in the Invader's presence, or I shall die."

Nina did not speak. She lay wide-eyed in the fluid that tickled through her lungs and across her every centimeter. Agape's floating form warmed her.

"The Invader is here," said Agape.

Nina saw nothing, but she felt Agape's warmth intensify, and brighten, and Rayn's distorted face began to reappear. Flesh filled in around his missing eyes and nose, and the convulsion stopped. He reached out for a second, eyes flickering in panic—

Nina reached out through Agape's body and touched Rayn's fingers.

He relaxed, and fell asleep.

Nina cried for hours before joining his rest.

* * *

Rayn awoke to the Invader's hand and shivered. His skin felt as if he'd bathed in warm milk after a long massage, and the Invader's face and chest wore new scars that glowed and glittered like topaz, ruby, and sapphire.

The Invader smiled. Rayn almost laughed in response—the Being looked shy and commanding all at once, like a wondering child and a knowing doctor in one, flowing around Rayn and Agape, a healing river of life in the cold of space.

"When you're done with me, I want to take away people's pain in the way you do," Rayn said. "I had no idea who you were—that you were this."

"It's never a fair fight, if you know me," said the Words. "To keep your free will, you have to decide on me before you know me. It's a challenging thing."

Rayn's vision cleared, and he could see stars spread like carpet around them. Agape curled around Rayn and Nina like a large cat now, or like a puddle of flannel blankets.

Nina!

Rayn's chest ached. He brushed her hair out of her sleeping face. She awoke.

"I'm sorry," he said to her.

"It's not your fault," she whispered. "I cannot give up my opportunity in Upper Synovi."

He swallowed a lump in his throat. "Will Agape be taking you straight to the adult level?"

"Yes, but I will not see him again. I do not trust the sprites—I am Neutral. And if the rumors are true at all, you will find that the sprites make happiness and health in Upper Synovi almost impossible. I'm not giving up my life for anyone."

Rayn allowed himself a weak smile. He touched her cheek. "They want me to finish my training in the youth level, and then return to Lower Synovi. Maybe I can rescue some others like me in the youth level first."

"Are you sure it worked?"

"What?"

"The heart change."

Rayn smirked. "They tell me it's a gradual thing. The first change is sudden, but then your whole self adapts to that change, and that's gradual. I don't know what they mean."

Nina closed her eyes, rolling over on her back. "I will miss you."

He bit his lip. He wanted to protest, to argue about the power of love, but could not.

"I thought about it, for a long time," she continued. "If you're serious about the Invader, you'll be trying to change hearts at every turn, including my own. You'll be practically and maybe even literally bathing in these Virtus that I hate."

"Your heart would be feeding the Prince, still," Rayn murmured.

"See, just you believing that makes my skin crawl. I will not go back with you to the juvenile level, and you cannot stay on the adult level with me, because you're literally in a war. I've lost you already."

*I've lost you already.* The words made Rayn want to weep. He closed both his hands around hers and just breathed, watching her face and enjoying her presence while he could. Perhaps she could not see the Invader because she had her eyes so tightly fixed on one prize. Perhaps she'd become so accustomed to injustice she could not recognize it to fight it. He did not know. He only knew that his chest ached around her.

They faded through the organic wall into an upper hallway. Agape lowered Nina onto the spongy floor. She extended her hand.

"Come with me, Rayn," she said. "You could *like* the Invader, from a distance, but not fight that war. You already got the heart change, right? So you're safe, right?"

"But if it's real, then how can I just let everyone else die?" Rayn stammered. "Could I live with you, and we just not talk about…" Even as he began to say it, he realized that would mean letting her die. It wouldn't be loving *her* to stay with her, holding his silence, pretending she didn't have anything wrong even as he became more and more aware of the heart disease; he would be using her to love *himself*.

Rayn shook his head, and laughed bitterly. This stream of thought would never have occurred to him before. "If I could go back to the way I was," he murmured. When modern medicine cured blindness, did people ever wish they could go back to not seeing?

No, they didn't. He gazed at her hand, seeing in it so many possibilities of a future that would never be, and back at the waiting Light that contained the Code for Everything.

"You have the strongest will, Nina," Rayn sighed. He brushed her hand away to embrace her and lingered in her arms, longing, wishing that somehow he could have followed his heart for her back in the warehouse without losing his heartbeat.

Then Agape swept him away and he was gone.

* * *

The day Rayn returned from his kidnapping, he walked against the crowd.

As the chip-tune music played, Rayn climbed back through the square hatch into his room and tumbled into the soft embrace of the gooey floor. He lay there the whole day, drifting in and out of deliriums about Nina and the Invader. Sleep teased him.

The day after he returned, the pitch of his heart rang up negative on the tube in the group lab.

"You got some kind of medical condition?" asked Wyn.

"I guess it's just who I am," Rayn answered. He glanced up at Voni, who acknowledged him with a nod.

That night, Rayn and Voni spoke out in the hallway until early morning, plotting to rescue their classmates from the Prince. Rayn discovered that he still couldn't be more different from the other Traitor; Voni's journey had driven him to become softer, but Rayn found himself somehow more warlike. Voni spoke at length about his fears for Upper Synovi's children, who grew up without older brothers and kindness, but Rayn most resented Lower Synovi, and the idea of anyone growing up like Nina had. He wanted to reverse whatever history had created that poverty. Did the pulsing of the hallways match the pulsing of the Prince's machine? What did Upper Synovi's living hallways *feed on*?

Sleep teased him that night, too, with visions of the meaning of hunger, of placing his hand on Nina's arm to take away the abrasion on her wrist, and of the child huddled in the trash on Nina's street. In his dreams, Rayn gave the child a name. Mason, he called him, Mason, and he wondered how often Mason got to eat, or whether or not Mason would ever touch any of the plants and pleasures and passions the hallways handed Rayn on a silver platter. And could Mason read?

And then, the smile of the Being who would solve it all, etched in thunderstorming, gale-forcing glory into a living mountain range of orange, yellow, and red-leaved trees…

"To form a friendship with a hurricane," he heard himself murmur.

But this hunger was sweet.

The third night after returning, Rayn gave up sleeping on the soft floor. He found a solid bit of plexiglass and some blankets, and rolled onto that, calling it a bed like she did. He closed his eyes and imagined the girl breathing in the hallway above his, curled around the disembodiment blaster she used to guard her mistrust. He reached out to hold her hand, and fell fast asleep.

He dreamt he could hear Nina's heartbeat from the hallway above.

* * *

So Wyn was an unremarkable jerk in a remarkable world. Every night while he slept the living hallways outside his room grew, creeping through his floating city to form the streets for tomorrow. Every morning the hallways clicked, Wyn's alarm beeped the chip-tune national anthem, and he tumbled out of bed, scurried like a hamster through his shower-tube, and stepped out his door into a new spongy corridor, dressed in the silver robe of an up-and-coming young professional.

This morning was remarkable because after his classes, Wyn's handsome but undeniably weird roommate stopped him in the hallway, blocking his path with one arm on either side of the doorway to their room.

"Hey. So I know Gineane's coming over tonight," Rayn said.

Wyn smirked and crossed his arms. "Yeah? What about it? She's mine now."

Rayn laughed, and shook his head. "No, see, that's what I wanted to talk to you about." He lowered his voice. "Look, I know this isn't how we think around here, but she's a human being. She doesn't belong to you. Don't treat her like something disposable. Listen to her. Treasure her. Find out how you can support her dreams. And for the love of God please don't brag about her private bedroom activities with the other guys around the table tomorrow."

Wyn scoffed. "S'not like you treated her any better."

"And that's why she left me."

"I don't want her around forever man, so that works out, too."

Rayn sighed, and rubbed his hands across the back of his head. "Well. She's worth more than that, and you're an asshole for not seeing what she really is."

"Imma what?"

"You're an asshole." Rayn shrugged, and his shrug infuriated Wyn. Wyn sized up against Rayn, towering over him, and threw out his chin.

"Say that again?" he asked.

"You heard me," Rayn said. "You treat every girl like she only exists for your personal amusement."

"Hey preachy, you wanna get locked out in the hallways again?"

Rayn laughed, and it bothered Wyn because he used to be the one who controlled Rayn's laughter. He always knew what caused it. He could count on Rayn's laugh.

And now it seemed alien. "You're getting weird, man," Wyn grumbled.

Rayn lowered his voice again, his eyes burning. "Well, I guess that's your fault. So if you don't feel like treating your girl right, I can go get a psych-eval that says exposure in the hallways messed with my brain. And, if you want, I can sue you with that psych-eval."

"Hold up, are you threatening me? For real?"

"No. I'm *asking* you not to treat her like you did this morning."

"I call it like I see it."

Rayn's eyebrows flickered. "Then I can have the civil authority call it like they see it, too." And just like that, he turned to go.

But where was he going? Wasn't he afraid of being locked out? Whose room would he stay in, instead?

Wyn shivered. He'd heard rumors that instead of taking the high-paying commercial position everyone expected, Rayn planned to start litigating for women who said they didn't "want it." And he'd heard Rayn talking with Voni about saving up cheques for something called "the Hungry."

It all sounded like some kind of horror movie. Wyn just wanted to ask what had happened to his old roommate, but he was utterly terrified that in some way he'd killed the man and brought back something else. A ghost from the hallways...

"Hey why do you even care?" Wyn blurted, yelling after Rayn to try to regain control. "She cheated on you! She *is* a whore!"

Rayn threw back a breezy smile over his shoulder. "People make mistakes, Wyn. And actually," he paused, laughing again. "If we want to get technical, out of the three of us, there's only one who's ever slept with someone for cash. And it's not her." Rayn pointed two fingers at Wyn. "Be good."

"No, no wait," Wyn stammered, then steadied his voice like the man he was. "Stop." He tried again and stomped. His bare foot *splurshed* in the soft tunnel floor. "Stop!"

Rayn paused. The patience on his face made Wyn want to punch him.

"No, I mean it," Wyn cried out. "This isn't you. Why do *you* care?"

Rayn's eyes softened.  A pain Wyn had never seen before streaked his face, and Rayn's deep breath took him aback. "I dunno, man," Rayn said. "I guess…

"I guess that's just who I am."


The End

# Also by Jen Finelli, MD

I hope you enjoyed what you just read! And if you didn't, well, it's over and you never have to go through that ever again!

But if you did, I actually send out a lot of free fiction either weekly or monthly at http://byjenfinelli.com/you-want-heroes-and-fairies/

And if you'd like to buy another book, you can do that below!

**Becoming Hero**
**SKYE** is the storm-tossed comic character out for revenge on the author who murdered his family.

**JACE** is the math-loving #blerd trying to escape his father's deadly legacy.

When their worlds collide, Jace must choose between the real world he's always hated, and the comic book world he's always loved–and Skye must decide if killing his author will save his world…or damn his soul.

Get the comic book character who challenges his author wherever books are sold! Full list of links at http://becominghero.ninja/

**NEODYMIUM EXODUS**

Lem's a mace-wielding teen space-ninja in a universe of sentient insectoids, purple jungles, and insane electromagnetic fields. She solves most problems by hitting harder, and never plays by her enemy's rules – until Jared Diebol captures her.

Diebol's the rising leader of an army uniting the galaxy by force. He believes the violent energy being Njande has "contaminated" Lem and her friends from another dimension, infiltrating their EEG signals to conquer the matter-based universe. The army usually kills contaminated people – but Diebol vows to cure Lem. When Diebol kidnaps Lem's family, he forces her to choose between the matter beings she loves and the energy person she adores. If Lem rejects Diebol's cure, her family dies – but if Lem cuts out Njande's energy, she opens our universe to a much darker thermodynamic attack.

A blend of hard biomedical science fiction with multicultural fantasy, Neodymium Exodus combines the introspection of classics like Perelandra with the vibrant boldness of modern best-sellers like This Alien Shore and Space Opera. Preorder with Wordfire Press for a bonus gift!

This series is probably the most important thing I've done in my life, and I am really excited to share it with the world. It's being traditionally published with Kevin J. Anderson's Wordfire Press, which has published SFWA presidents and even work from *Dune* author Frank Herbert–I am really honored to be in such proud company, and I really hope you'll get a copy. Make sure to stay in touch here so you know when it's live: http://byjenfinelli.com/the-neodymium-universe/

**Origins: A Guardian Anthology**

A Puerto Rican engineering student battles Multiple Sclerosis–and experiments with dangerous body modifications. A girl in a red hijab leaps into the flames of a rotting convenience store–to save someone who hates her. An Asian-American 9th-grader catches a doctor poisoning his city's water supply to "cure" cancer. An Irish-American kid scarred by his alcoholic father turns his own broken, twisted psychology into a super-weapon. A restless Black girl from the South uncovers a human trafficking ring, and as she navigates the complexities of police-victim relationships, she roots out a conspiracy that could change her planet forever.

This neurodiverse, ethnically open anthology uncovers the origins of the Guardian superhero team from the highly-anticipated Becoming Hero comic-within-a-novel. Based on real teen struggles, these stories follow the team's creation as new heroes are born, built, broken, and forged.  Head here to get the book: http://byjenfinelli.com/origins-the-guardian-anthology/

**Prometheus Studies**

In Greek mythology, Prometheus created mankind and saved them from cold ignorance by bringing them fire. As punishment for helping humans, whom the evil rapist Zeus hated, Prometheus was bound to the top of a high mountain. There, alone for centuries but for the comfort of a passing female traveler, bitter wind gnawed at his naked flesh while every day an eagle came to feast on his liver. Suffering man, yet eternal God, pierced in his side, exposed and alone for the salvation of humanity…like Yeshua, called by the Gentiles Jesus, who died to bring fire to our hearts.

Physician and science fiction author Jen Finelli believes God leaves behind traces of pure Awesome in places we usually don't look. We are here to pick up the little glimmers and put them together: to study, through tarantulas, photons, Pilobilus, whatever, the true Prometheus and the fire that is life.

This is not a book about religious or scientific debate, but a daily series of mystic inspiration found in plants, DNA, vectors, and more.

Buy now from for a bonus gift inside, or enjoy five days of secret podcasts, preview meditations, and extra gifts, without spending a cent! Head here for the goodies: http://byjenfinelli.com/prometheus-studies/